KINGSTON

AND THE

ECHOES OF MAGIC

KINGSTON

AND THE
ECHOES OF MAGIC

RUCKER MOSES
AND THEO GANGI

putnam

G. P. PUTNAM'S SONS

G. P. PUTNAM'S SONS

An imprint of Penguin Random House LLC, New York

Copyright © 2021 by Craig S. Phillips and Harold Hayes, Jr.
Map and interior illustrations © 2021 by Sienne Josselin

Visit us online at penguinrandomhouse.com

Library of Congress Cataloging-in-Publication Data
Names: Moses, Rucker, author. | Gangi, Theo, author. | Moses, Rucker.
Kingston and the magician's lost and found.
Title: Kingston and the echoes of magic / Rucker Moses and Theo Gangi.
Description: New York: G. P. Putnam's Sons, [2021] | Summary: When his magician father's old rival, Maestro, finds a way to overwrite reality with an alternate timeline in which he rules over all, Kingston, Too Tall, and V must find a way into the Realm and travel back through time to stop Maestro and save Brooklyn before it is erased for good.
Identifiers: LCCN 2021022305 (print) | LCCN 2021022306 (ebook)
ISBN 9780525516897 (hardcover) | ISBN 9780525516903 (ebook)
Subjects: CYAC: Magic—Fiction. | Reality—Fiction. | Time travel—Fiction.
Family life—Brooklyn (New York, N.Y.)—Fiction. | Magicians—Fiction.
African Americans—Fiction. | Brooklyn (New York, N.Y.)—Fiction.
Classification: LCC PZ7.1.M67725 Ki 2021 (print)
LCC PZ7.1.M67725 (ebook) | DDC [Fic]—dc23
LC record available at https://lccn.loc.gov/2021022305
LC ebook record available at https://lccn.loc.gov/2021022306

Printed in the United States of America
ISBN 9780525516897
1 3 5 7 9 10 8 6 4 2
CJKV

Design by Suki Boynton • Text set in Warnock Pro

I'VE BEEN HERE before.

Every sight and every sound feel as familiar as yesterday.

Whenever that was.

We're riding the subway home from the Barclays Center. I got a seat by the window. It's Friday evening, and Christmas is just days away. The Brooklyn Nets just lost to the New York Knicks. *The thum-da-doom* of the tracks rumbles in my bones. All the heads of all the passengers bob to the rhythm. My eyes are drifting shut. I'm sleepy from all the shouting and popcorn eating and Milly Rocking during time-outs. I stare out the dark glass. The tunnel speeds along, and sharp dashes of light blast by like laser beams.

The subway window reflects the inside of the car. I can see my best bud Too Tall, my primo prima Veronica, and my uncle Crooked Eye, dead asleep and snoring. And there's myself looking right back at me. High cheekbones. Hair twists growing long up top.

The subway lights flash off. It's pitch-dark, and then light again.

As we roll into Ricks Street, my uncle's eyes snap open like he's got some kind of sixth subway sense, and he's awake and talking.

But I know what he's going to say before he says it.

Let's go, sleepyfaces.

"Let's go, sleepyfaces. It's our stop."

You're one to talk, Unc.

"You're one to talk, Unc," says Veronica, standing and steadying herself as the train slows to a stop. "You snore louder than the express train."

As we exit the train, file through the turnstiles, and climb the staircase to the street, I'm thinking about how the first thing I'll see on the horizon is the Black Rock of BK, as the news started calling it. The hard crystal rock that's encased what was formerly the Mercury Theater and is now the main tourist attraction of Echo City. There's even this federal Omega team from the government that's investigating it. They've got tents set up around the Mercury, and they wear these orange vests with the letter *O* on the back. I guess they're trying to figure out what it is and what it's doing here and why all the blackouts, but they can't explain it. I know because I happen to be one of the very few who actually sorta can.

This past summer, a big rift from another dimension called the Realm heaped out tons of raw energy that immediately crystalized into a huge, towering rock, like a mountain right smack-dab on the streets of Brooklyn.

I can imagine how the rock will look when I get up to the street—the sunset glowing pink and the black crystal looking down on the brownstone roofs, shadow long in the streets like it's on stilts.

Once I reach aboveground and check the skyline, I see how exactly right I was. The Black Rock of BK is just how I pictured. But only for a moment.

The sun soon settles all the way down, and the darkness grows and spills into the shadows of alleys and buildings. Then the lights go out. Blackness pours over us like somebody knocked an ink bottle over on Echo City.

Then the streetlamps pop back on with a flicker.

"Whoa," says Too Tall with a squint. "These outages are a trip, boy." He zips his bubble coat up and pulls his skullcap over his ears, like the lights going out made it colder somehow.

I wait a second and then raise my gloved hand.

"Let there be . . . *dark*," I say as the streetlights dim and go out again, the way they do when you're close to the Mercury.

It feels even darker than last time.

"King, you're really freaking us out, you know? If you're doing this, could you stop, please?" he asks, looking at my gloved hand. "What I mean is"—he clears his throat and drops his voice an octave deeper—"I'm not scared of the dark at all."

"Not at all," says Veronica.

But I'm not doing it. I just know when it will happen. Because I've been here before.

↯

ONE THING I like about when the lights go out in the city: You can actually see the stars. Most of the time, I forget about them. In Brooklyn, there's so much to see at eye level: stores, cars, outfits, faces, WALK/DON'T WALK signs, bus stops, buildings, brownstones, yards, stairs, doorways. There's even a ton to see when you look down. For one, people's feet—Brooklyn's sneaker game is out of control. Sometimes you just need to look down because the sidewalks crack different. Trees *do* grow in Brooklyn; they grow big and the roots break the sidewalk, so you'd better watch your step. You never really look up. There's no reason to. With the glare of streetlamps and holiday lights and the dome of smog, you usually can't see the stars even if you want to.

But since the outages, I've been looking up more and more. Especially now that it's winter and it gets dark so early. It reminds me of when we used to visit Grandpa Freddy in Georgia. You could really see the stars out there. Pops used to stare up at them. He'd call it Little Big Sky.

I look up now and think, *When the lights go out, Brooklyn's got its own Little Big Sky.* Thousands of tiny lights surrounded by infinite blackness. I don't know the stars too well. But I look for the ones I do know—the three points of Orion's Belt. Something about it always makes me think of the Realm.

Maybe it's because Pops is in the Realm, and I want to get him home.

Or maybe it's because of what it was like when I was in the Realm.

I jumped from echo to echo to echo, like the three

stars in Orion's Belt, and in between was black and vast, like the space that surrounds the stars.

Looking out into space, I feel small. Not just me, but my house and family and my block and city, even. Everything I know is so small compared with the humongous galaxy.

But another part of me feels like, *I was in the night sky*. Like, *out there* in some wild interdimensional convergence of outer or inner space. And that makes me feel big. Big as the whole universe sometimes.

"WANNA GO GRAB dinner over at King's Cup?" suggests Veronica as the streetlights come back on.

She's talking about the café my mom opened up on the ground floor of our family brownstone. She named it King's Cup after yours truly.

"Nah," I say, "probably out of real food by now anyways. Just down to pastries. Let's hit Not Not Ray's. Matteo's got those holiday cannoli with the green and red sprinkles."

"Mmm, sprinkles," says Tall.

"Thought you said you didn't just want pastries," Veronica says.

"I mean after we eat the pizza, of course," I say.

"*Mmm, pizza,*" says Tall.

"It's your world, kids," says Uncle Crooked like Brooklyn's own Santa Claus.

Not Not Ray's pizza oven blazes with warmth at any time of year, but it's especially satisfying when those cold winds blow outside. Right away we unbutton coats, unzip hoodies, unwrap scarves, and yank off gloves. Except my one white glove. The one that covers my otherwise invisible Realm hand. The hand that got stuck in another dimension and sort of *stayed there.* I mean, I can still use the hand, but without the glove, it's invisible to the eye. So this glove stays on, always. Don't want to freak out the Brooklynites.

Soon enough, Matteo serves a steaming pie full of glowing pepperoni, oil pooling in the little red circles. We thank him, and the conversation goes quiet as all our mouths are promptly full of cheesy, crust-crunchy bites.

"You got something against the crust?" Veronica asks Too Tall as bits of crust pile up on his plate like chicken bones.

"By *crust,* do you mean *pepperoni-and-sauce-and-cheese-less dough*?" Too Tall replies.

"Uh, I guess. Never quite thought of it that way."

Too Tall taps a finger to his temple.

"But the crust is delicious," says Uncle Crooked Eye, chomping on crust ends like bread sticks.

"Let me ask you this, Mr. Crooked: When we buy a pizza pie, do we pay for the cheese and meat slices and sauce? Or do we pay for the dough?"

"Some of us don't pay for anything," mutters Veronica.

"Hey, Tall, what do you say to movie night tonight?" I ask, thinking, for some reason, that he might say yes this time.

"No can do."

"Egypt again?"

"Ancient Egypt again," he confirms.

"Homework for the holidays? What happened to Christmas spirit?" says Crooked Eye, pizza sauce dribbling off his lip. "I'll give you some homework—how 'bout using that giant frame of yours to help me hang some lights? Homework will be forgotten, but the Christmas light show at King's Cup tomorrow night, *that* will go down in history."

Veronica snorts soda out of her nose as we all laugh at Crooked Eye's bold pronouncement.

"School these days trying to turn you kids into serious little study robots," he goes on. "You need time to play."

Crooked is probably the only adult I know who feels this way.

"Well, it's not exactly homework," says Tall. "It's a make-up assignment, since I failed my Egypt paper first go-round."

"You *failed*?" asks Veronica. "Wasn't my dad helping you with that?"

"He sure was. Mr. Cruikshank put so much red ink on that thing, I thought his pen was leaking. Went and talked to him after, and he said my whole paper was wrong. Only thing I got right was my name."

Veronica bites her lip. "You should go tell my father," she says.

"Pass," says Too Tall. "Long Fingers scares me. I'm not about to tell him he's wrong about anything."

"Uncle Long Fingers isn't wrong about stuff like that," I say.

Too Tall holds his hands up. "I don't care who's wrong. I just want to pass."

Crooked Eye shakes his head. "And that's also what's wrong with you kids nowadays. No appreciation for knowledge."

"Nobody knows anything, Uncle Crooked," says Veronica. "Google it."

"Some folks know things," says Crooked Eye, but V is so convincing, he doesn't sound entirely sure.

I say under my breath, "Three . . . two . . . one . . ."

Right on cue, there's a blackout. Not Not Ray's and the streets go dark.

The lights come right back on, and everyone is blinking to adjust.

"Wish somebody knew—why the blackouts?" says Matteo Spinelli from behind the counter. "Hafta keep restarting my dishwasher." He shakes his head.

I shrug and have at my pizza slice.

Once we finish, Matteo comes over with a plate of fresh cannoli, with red and green Christmas sprinkles decorating the filling. He whistles like a bomb is dropping and sets the plate down with a *boom*. Our faces go bright as Times Square.

"Special holiday treat for you. Say, have you all seen that new mural? A holiday portrait of Echo City down on the back of the old Davenport Brothers Furniture store. Che bello, beautiful. I took my son there last night."

"Haven't seen it yet, Matteo," I say. "I'll check it out for sure."

Everyone nods as greedy hands reach across the table for the plate of cannoli.

"Can't wait to cap off all that cheese and crust with cheese and crust but sweet this time," says Veronica.

Matteo is still standing there, smiling at me.

He wants a magic trick.

I give him a wink and a nod.

We polish off those cannoli like a school of piranhas. There isn't a crumb or sprinkle left. The wax sheet on the plate barely survived.

As we put our coats on, I eye Matteo's tip jar, with the words *We Knead the Dough* written on it. I run a quarter up and down my white-gloved fingers. I let everyone file out in front of me and thank Matteo by flicking the quarter with my thumb. It soars across the shop, over the tables, chairs, and counter, to plop like a raindrop into his tip cup. I step outside to his ringing applause.

He catches me halfway down the block, thanks me, and hands me a paper bag. Three cannoli are inside.

"Thanks, Matteo!"

"Dibs on one," says Veronica as we head toward home.

"Can I, um, bug you for one of the other ones?" asks Too Tall.

"Long as you don't mind carrying it without a bag," I say.

Too Tall takes a cannoli in his crane-like hand, bumps a fist to mine, and peels off to do homework. Crooked Eye walks up ahead, so Veronica and I are side by side.

"V, you ever get the sense that everything that's happening has happened already?"

"Like déjà vu?" she says.

"I guess. Why's it called that?"

"Think it's French for 'already seen,'" says V.

"Is there a French word for that, but, like, even stronger?"

"Most likely, though I don't speak French. Is something bothering you?"

I shrug. "It's just like all the days are so . . . the *same*. You know what I'm saying?"

I turn and look at her. I realize I really want to know if she knows what I mean. And I've never asked her this before. Guess not everything tonight has happened already.

"I dunno, sometimes, maybe?"

"But not now?"

She thinks about it, and then something clicks, and her eyes narrow. "Are you saying you're experiencing some bad déjà vu right now?"

"You could say that."

"I was just reading about this on this website about insomnia."

"When were you reading that?"

"When I couldn't sleep one night, genius. There are a few possibilities. First question: Do you believe in past lives?"

"I guess anything's possible. But not really, no."

"All right, well, are you sleeping enough?" she asks.

"Not exactly."

"Well, there you go. Could be 'cause you're groggy, and when you're groggy, things always seem same-y. Or, when you did sleep, you had precog dreams."

"Precog?"

"Yeah. Like, your dreams predict the future. So things feel like they've already happened to you because they sorta *did*—in your dreams."

"I don't know. I never really remember my dreams."

"Okay, well, have you heard of the tuning fork phenomenon?"

"Did you say *fork*?"

"Yeah, it's when your brain is tuned in to frequencies from, like, other dimensions. Temporarily."

I don't say anything. But she might be hitting closer to the truth with that one.

"I'm sure you just need more sleep. Most of us do. But here's something you can try. If your dreams are feeling lucid—like, super real—or reality is feeling super dreamy, do this: Every time you walk through a doorway, whether in dreams or reality, touch the doorway and say to yourself, 'I'm not dreaming.'"

"What? Why would I do that?"

"Because it can make you, like, more *aware*. If you're getting really bad déjà vu, your mind might be trying to tell you something. Just try it, okay?"

We hit the James brownstone with sleepy walks and slow yawns. We watch old Christmas movies on TV until Ma gets home. She takes off her shoes and crashes on the couch. Another big day at King's Cup Café. She's buzzing with the rush of how busy it was. She talks about all the customers, how she barely had time to breathe. Then she falls asleep right there before I can give her the cannoli I saved for her.

I watch a few shows and take myself to bed. After I brush my teeth, I head to my room. On the way, I touch the doorway and say out loud, "I'm not dreaming."

3

"**WHAT DO YOU** mean, *this has all happened before?*" asks
Too Tall, setting an empty soda can down on the sidewalk.
"I just had this brilliant idea for how to help you control
your powers yesterday," he insists, pointing to the can.

"It's hard to explain, Tall. It's just like I've experienced
this before and know what's about to happen next."

Tall takes a step back from the can. A couple of weeks
ago, I reached out for a soda can with my Realm hand,
but before I could touch it, the can imploded. Fizzy-malt
soda burst in the air and got me all wet and sticky. Too
Tall has been obsessed ever since. He thinks if I can crush
a can on the sidewalk from up on the stoop, I can do anything. "Now . . . *Kingston crush!*" he says, and makes a fist.

I focus on the soda can and curl my fingers into a fist with my Realm hand.

"Crush!" he says again.

Only, the soda can sits whole on the sidewalk, taunting us, uncrushed and undefeated.

"I get it, you need smoke or fog or some physical object, like you did that time in the theater," Tall says as his shoulders slump, and he joins me back on the stoop.

"I don't think it's like that. I just have to concentrate and it's like my hand can be anywhere. But I can't always seem to find the focus," I say.

I've got his cell phone. I start typing something on the notepad app.

"Did you know that wasn't going to work?" he asks.

"I had a hunch," I admit.

He looks over my shoulder to see what I'm typing, but I move away. "Well, you are a magical dude and all. So maybe you can see the future?" he suggests.

"Yeah, Veronica says maybe I'm having lucid dreams." I explain to him how she told me to touch every doorway and say "I'm not dreaming" to myself.

"And?" he asks.

"Well, I'm trying it. Everything is still super familiar, but I think I remembered my dream last night, and that's new."

"Yeah?"

"Yeah." I can tell Too Tall is on the fence about whether to ask what I dreamed about. Like it's too personal.

"I dreamed about my dad," I say. "He was trapped in an echo. Doing the same thing over and over. And he couldn't get out."

Tall nods to me. "Yeah. Guess that sounds about right, huh?"

"Guess so."

Thing is, Pops really *is* trapped in an echo—a loop of twenty-six hours—in the Realm.

Last time I saw my dad, he was trying to find his way home to our reality. We were in the Mercury Theater. I held his hand. And then Urma Tan, aka the She-Wizard of Torrini Boulevard, showed up, and everything went wrong. She turned the whole Mercury Theater into a giant crystal, and I had to break the portal just to send her back to the Realm for good.

But in the process, we lost Dad to the Realm. Now it's like he's farther away than ever before.

"You remember when my dad had that knee surgery?" asks Tall. "He was home for months trying to get right. And then my knees started hurting? Like real bad, couldn't even get up and down the court?"

I nod.

"Your ma said it was sympathy pains," says Tall. "Think maybe that's what's going on with you?"

"Sympathy pains? Like, I feel like I'm on repeat 'cause I know my dad is somewhere, on repeat?"

He shrugs. "I guess? Oh wait, look," he whispers, eyeing a couple of girls he kind of knows coming down the block. "I got an idea. You can't crush the can, right, because there's no pressure! Maybe all those times you used your powers this summer, you could 'cause you were under the gun. Mint's boys had us or Urma was 'bout to get us. You're a magician, so you need to perform! Try with these girls here. Now, when they get up close, crush the can with your powers. Oh, and gimme my phone. I'll record you. More pressure," he says, winking.

I sigh. Here we go again.

The two girls come down the block, both wearing all-white Uptowns, one pair clean, the other pair not-so.

I hand the phone over. He sets it down on the step beneath us and starts recording the soda can on the sidewalk.

The two girls come closer, popping gum and laughing about something. When they are almost at the soda can, Tall whispers to me, *"Now!"*

I close my Realm hand into a fist.

The soda can instantly crushes in on itself with a *crunch*.

The two girls nearly jump out of their shoes.

"Oh my god, my heart just stopped," says one, holding a hand to her chest.

"Did you see that?" the other asks me and Tall.

"See what?" says Tall.

The girls keep walking, staring warily at the crushed soda can.

"You did it! That was amazing!" Tall says once they're out of sight.

He grabs his phone to check out the recording. Then he looks at me and pauses. "What? You telling me you saw all that coming?"

"Just look in your notepad app," I say.

Too Tall scrolls over to the app and reads what I just wrote out loud.

"'Oh my god my heart just stopped, says clean Uptowns,'" he reads. "'Did you see that? says dirty Uptowns. See what? says Too Tall.'"

He closes his phone and frowns. "Thank you, Mr. Magicman Killjoy."

The door to my home opens behind us.

My uncle Long Fingers roars out of the doorway. He squints in the sun like it's been a while since he's seen it. There's chalky spittle on the sides of his mouth like he's frothing with rage. "*Who says* my answers were all wrong?"

Although this is all super familiar, it's still amazing to see Long Fingers get so close to leaving the brownstone. Veronica is grinning behind him.

Too Tall stutters, "I—uh—it's not my fault, Uncle Long! Mr. Cruikshank, he said the dates in my answers were wrong by about eight thousand years! He said to use the textbook!"

Long Fingers growls and paces at the edge of the doorway like a caged big cat. "*Textbook*? Hah! Quackademics know nothing about ancient Egypt. The Egyptians invented magic, but do they ask magicians anything? Of course not. Just 'archaeologists' and 'Egyptologists.'" Long Fingers throws up angry quotation fingers. "They probably think the sphinx is just a few thousand years old, am I right?"

Too Tall winces and prepares for heavy fire. "Yeah?"

"You get that paper. You bring it back here," Long Fingers instructs. "We will prepare our rebuttal."

My uncle storms back inside.

Veronica stands in the doorway, biting her lip. Once we hear another door slam from inside the house, she busts out laughing.

"King," says Too Tall, "if I ever ask your uncle for help with my homework again, please magic my mouth shut, okay?"

THAT EVENING, VERONICA and I are bundled up on the stoop, watching Uncle Crooked hook the last string of lights around the base of a lamppost. Crooked Eye has been laying Christmas lights on the stoop and the storefront all week to unveil his Saturday-night light show. He even found a plastic reindeer at a stoop sale, but Mom made him chuck it out back, saying it wasn't the right "look" for a "chic" coffee shop like King's Cup. Crooked made up for it by getting reams of lights up on the lamppost, the NO PARKING sign, the other NO PARKING sign, the phone lines, and even the fire hydrant, shooing the dogs away. All week he's been bragging about the power Long Fingers was going to generate to light up the whole block. "Like a supernova," he says.

"For Christmas?" I ask.

"A Christmas supernova," he confirms.

Mom is closing up shop. I realize we better go rescue Too Tall from Uncle Long Fingers's lecture on ancient Egypt.

My long-limbed friend sits on the couch beside our bookcase wall, staring at his laptop, which is covered with Hypebeast stickers. Long Fingers paces behind the couch. He rarely moves around, so this feels like an athletic event for him. He's talking in that heavy and deliberate way of his, like he's laying bricks one at a time.

"No, no, ancient Egyptians did not *think* there was life after death. They were not superstitious buffoons and savages, like your textbook says. Egyptians *discovered* how to achieve a higher state of consciousness and become a *celestial entity*," Uncle Long says with absolute certainty, and waits for Too Tall to write it down.

"Uncle Fingers, I don't think Mr. Cruikshank is going to go for that answer."

"Young Tall, do you want a mere grade, or to understand Truth with a capital *T*?"

"Honestly? You may not think it to look at me, Uncle Fingers, sir, but I get good grades, and I kinda want to keep it that way."

"Yeah, Uncle Long," I say, feeling bad for Too Tall. "School just makes us jump through hoops, you know? Best to just tell them what they want to hear."

Uncle Long Fingers looks at me, deeply disappointed.

First he says to Too Tall, "If you weren't a smart boy, I wouldn't waste my breath." Then he comes around the couch to look at me face-to-face. "Young King, we are more than flesh, blood, and bone. You of all people should know that." He puts a hand on my shoulder. "*We are luminous beings.* All of us. Understand?"

I nod slowly.

Uncle Long and I have a funny relationship. He knows more about me and magic than anyone. He knows about my trip through the Realm and my magic hand. Sometimes he tries to teach me about magic, but he makes it sound so abstract, it's hard to follow. Like, *we are luminous beings.* What's that supposed to mean? Why should I, *of all people*, understand? Sometimes it's like he's not talking to me at all, but rather my dad.

"Light-show time!" V jumps in. "Uncle Crooked wants us out front," she says, rescuing everyone. Maybe she's sorry about telling her father that Too Tall has to redo his paper.

"Speaking of luminous. Adjourned, Young Tall. We will continue," says Long Fingers.

Out on the front stoop, Crooked Eye lines us up on the sidewalk for his big reveal, talking loud enough for Long Fingers to hear him inside as he works the circuits to his custom power generator. Or at least that's Long Fingers's excuse for not coming outside.

"Nina, Veronica, King," Crooked Eye says in his stage voice, glancing to each of us. "And Mr. Tall. It's been years since we've had occasion to fire up the ole Christmas lights. Now we've got a full house and the most *poppingest* café in the neighborhood. So it's a perfect time to light up the street for the holiday. Ladeeez and gentlemenz, Dyker Heights ain't got nothin' on me!"

Crooked Eye throws his hands in the air and crosses his eyes as Long Fingers flicks the switch from inside the house.

Christmas lights everywhere—in the trees, around the windows, across the sidewalk, on the traffic lights—light up as bright as a lightning strike.

And about as brief.

In an instant, the lights are all gone.

And I mean *all* of them.

It's a blackout. Dark as the day is long.

Long Fingers shouts something. I can't quite make it out, but it sounds like bad words.

Crooked Eye rushes inside.

Then the lights come back on. The normal city lights, anyway. Crooked Eye's Christmas lights are still out.

Crooked Eye comes back out on the stoop, big grin showing teeth.

"Well, it was a very festive fraction of a second or so, Heyward," my mom says. She starts slow-clapping, and we all join in.

"Heh heh. Thanks, Nina. I think. It turns out, whatever happened to the power—not our fault, by the way—it fried Long Fingers's Tesla coil. Seeing as Harry's is closed, who's up for a subway ride to the late-night hardware store?"

I volunteer. V and Tall tag along.

$$\text{⚡}$$

As the four of us wait for the train, Crooked Eye blames the dead generator on his brother. Says he's not careful enough. "You know, our daddy used to tell us, *Y'all need discipline.*" Crooked imitates his father's southern accent. "He'd say, *I didn't know my daddy, Lawrence, you lucky you got me here to tell you—y'all need discipline,*" he says as if he's scolding Long Fingers.

The subway comes screeching down the tracks like a velociraptor. Brakes spark, and it stops with a dragon-size exhale. Doors open. We file onto the car and find seats. Veronica touches the doorway and whispers something. The doors close. The train moans and runs and hums.

And I've been here before.

The *thum-da-doom* of the tracks rumbles in my bones. All the heads of all the passengers bob to the rhythm. I stare out the dark glass. We speed through the tunnel, and sharp dashes of light blast by like laser beams.

The subway window holds the reflection of the inside of the car. I can see my best bud Too Tall, my primo prima Veronica, and my uncle Crooked Eye, dead asleep and snoring. I can see myself looking right back at me.

The subway lights flash off. It's pitch-dark, and then light again.

My uncle breaks me out of it. As we roll into Ricks Street, his eyes snap open like he's got some kind of sixth subway sense, and he's awake and talking.

But I know what he's going to say before he says it.

Let's go, sleepyfaces.

"Let's go, sleepyfaces. It's our stop."

You're one to talk, Unc . . .

I'm expecting the words to fly from V's mouth. But I don't hear them.

I turn to my cousin.

She's grilling me.

"Kingston," she says. "I've been here before!"

As we get off the train, Veronica can't contain herself.

"Okay, are we all just going to act like we didn't just get on the train at Ricks Street, turn around, and get off the train at Ricks Street?"

Too Tall and Crooked Eye look at V like she's lost every last marble.

"Um, you mean Barclays Center?" says Tall.

"Yeah, that's all she meant—get on and get off, what a fast ride, huh?" I say as we file out the turnstiles.

"What are you talking about?" she asks, eyeing my wheat Timbs, green bomber, and hoodie. "Those aren't even the same clothes." Then she checks her own outfit from yesterday, and she shrieks.

I take V by the elbow and whisper, "V, we don't need to freak everybody out."

"Are you sure?" she says, loud.

"Yes! No—I don't know," I say. "I sorta thought I was imagining it until just now."

"What do you mean? You told me yesterday—wait, I mean today? After we ate Not Not Ray's and Matteo gave you the cannoli and—oh my god, that hasn't even happened yet, has it?"

I shake my head.

V rubs the shaved part of her head with her fingertips like she's trying to make sense of where and when we are, exactly.

"I told you it feels like a dream," I say.

"I mean, I get why this may be happening to you, with your hand and all. But why is it happening to me? Tweedledee and Tweedledum seem clueless," she says, motioning toward Crooked Eye and Too Tall. "Why me?"

It's a good question. I mean, we are related. Her dad's been to the Realm just like mine. So, maybe it's a James thing? But why doesn't Ma or Crooked or Long Fingers remember?

"King, this is what it's been like for you? You just keep living the same day?"

"I guess. I don't *know*, V, it's like I get to the same moment, and I know it's happened already, but part of me forgets, you know? Part of me is totally *in it*, in each moment, as if it never happened. But part of me—"

"You guys coming?" Crooked Eye calls down from the top of the subway stairs.

Veronica and I have been exchanging rapid whispers in front of the subway booth.

"We have to get rid of them," she says, and marches up the stairs.

I follow her.

So this is really real, I think as the streets go dark. *It's not all in my head.*

"Okay, wow, what a crazy blackout, huh?" V says to Crooked Eye. "So dark! Say, Unc." Veronica yawns. "I'm feeling kinda tired, what say we skip dinner and just head home, how 'bout that?"

Tall and Crooked are caught a little off guard, but it's Veronica, so they're used to not knowing what she'll say or do next. We say good night to Tall, who looks particularly hungry for a cannoli as he shambles off.

We head home. V and I grab a couple croissants from the café before Mom throws them out and go upstairs. My room is a mess. Clothes in one corner like a pile of leaves.

Threadbare books I borrowed from Long Fingers's library stacked in another. The laptop Ma passed down to me last summer sits on the edge of my bed. My desk is littered with playing cards, coins, sketch pads, and journals.

On the wall above the desk, though, is one thing that's always straight and always clean. The framed poster of Pops, Preston the Great. A lightning bolt in one hand and cards in the other. His classic porkpie hat on his head. My uncles took it off the wall downstairs before Ma and I arrived. After everything that happened this past summer, Ma had Crooked Eye put it up in my room.

Dad, I think. It always comes back to him. Every time the world turns and my stomach lurches because something happens that can't be explained by logic or reason, he's there, somewhere, the magician just offstage.

Veronica jumps onto my bed and turns to me with a flake of pastry on her lip.

"So, do I have to say it?"

"Say what?" I ask.

"We're in an echo. I mean, right? We got on the train, maybe four o'clock or so, Friday evening. We get back on the train, what? Six o'clock, on Saturday? Do I have to count?"

"Twenty-six hours," I say.

In the Realm, there are all these echoes of realities. Moments in time that loop over and over. Those echoes are full of copies of people, created every time a portal to the Realm opens, living life exactly as they did in those twenty-six hours surrounding that moment.

"In an echo, like Dad. But how? I mean, unless . . ."

"Unless we are echoes of ourselves and not actually ourselves?" she asks.

We take that thought in for a moment.

"Um, maybe?" I say.

"But I remember my whole life!" says Veronica.

"I think echo people do, too," I say.

"But they never realize they're in an echo. They never wake up. We did."

"What changed for you? How did you wake up?" I ask.

"It's weird. Remember you asked me about déjà vu and all that?"

"Yeah, I think that's the first time I did that. I think every time before that we just talked about how much we like cannolis."

"Interesting. Well, remember I suggested you touch every doorway and say 'I'm not dreaming' out loud?"

"Yeah. I tried that."

"So did I. Not sure why, just thought it'd be cool if I

had a lucid dream, you know? Like, if you're aware you're dreaming, you could maybe control it and fly around like a bird?"

"Did it work?" I ask.

"I don't know. I don't remember my dreams at all. But then we get on the train at Ricks Street and I touch the doors and whisper, 'I'm not dreaming,' and next thing I know, we're getting off the train at Ricks Street!"

"So it worked. It woke you up, anyway."

"Maybe we need to wake everyone up?" suggests Veronica.

"Maybe," I say, staring up at my poster of Pops. "The way I figure it, we have two options."

"And those are?"

"One, we're echoes of ourselves. We just woke up some-how. In which case, we're better off going back to sleep."

"You think?"

"Yeah, V. Remember what happened to Urma Tan when she left her echo?"

"Yeah. That wasn't good. At all."

An echo of Urma Tan slipped into our reality. To stay alive outside the Realm, she had to wear a charged Realm crystal around her neck at all times. She lived here, had a kid, but it was a bad look all around. She drained her son like a vampire, then opened a Realm portal and tried to absorb so much Realm energy that, when she lost control, it covered the whole theater and crystalized into the Black Rock of BK.

"I don't really wanna go back to sleep," says V. "What's the other option?"

"The other option is, we're in an echo loop somehow. And we gotta figure it out. Otherwise, remember this day you just lived? Well, get used to it."

"**WHAT DO YOU** mean, 'this has all happened before'?" asks Too Tall, setting an empty soda can down on the sidewalk.

Strange how, even when you know you're trapped in a loop, you still can't help doing the same thing again and again. Like we're so programmed, and we don't even know.

Veronica and I stayed up late last night, trying to think of answers, but came up empty. I was so sleepy when I woke up that when Tall swung by, the most natural thing in the world was to hang out on the stoop in the bright, cold morning.

"Just forget it," I say. "Let's play your stupid sidewalk game."

Too Tall looks hurt. "You think it's stupid?"

"Sorry, Tall. I'm just frustrated."

"With?"

"You ever had a problem you know you're supposed to fix, but you have no clue what to do?"

"Ah," says a knowing Too Tall. "A phantom shoe pebble."

"Huh?"

"Like when you got something in your sock, it hurts when you step—"

"Exactly—"

"Only you take off your shoe, turn it upside down, tap it, turn your sock inside out, but no dice."

I nod. "And, like, no one else but me can fix this. It's my shoe. My sock. I feel the pain in my foot. So why can't I make it right?"

"Dunno what's bugging you, King, but we're not talking about shoe pebbles, are we?" Tall asks.

I shake my head.

"Sounds like a lot of pressure to put on a single person," he offers. "Maybe take it easy on yourself?"

For some reason, that sounds like the worst advice I've ever heard.

"But, Tall. It hurts when I walk."

He looks at my gum sole, tapping restlessly on the stoop.

"You don't mean that literally, right?"

The door slams open behind us.

"A mural!"

It's V, with her eyes wide.

"A what now?" says Tall.

"A new mural, King! Don't you remember?" she says, ignoring Tall.

"A what? Where?"

"Remember, when we ate at Not Not Ray's last night, he—"

"We didn't eat at Not Not Ray's," says Tall, bewildered. "I had to heat up week-old everything fried rice last night. And you *know* how hard it is to microwave rice."

"No, not *last* night," says Veronica. "The *last* last night."

"You're saying you ate at Not Not Ray's last last night?" says Tall. "Is it possible to see double, but with your ears?"

"You mean the *other* last night?" I ask her.

Too Tall puts a hand to his chest like I just betrayed him. "You too?"

Veronica holds up a finger and says, "Tall, we'll explain it to you in just a moment. Let the adults talk."

"Okay, you two are most definitely not adult—"

"King." Veronica's wide eyes beam back on me. "Remember Matteo said, 'Say, have you all seen that new mural? A holiday portrait of Echo City down on the back of the old Davenport Brothers Furniture store.'"

"Okay," I say. "So?"

"So it's probably one of *Sol's murals.*"

"Okay . . ."

Sol is the son of Urma Tan's echo self. He gets these wild visions of the Realm and paints murals of what he sees. Pretty reliable way to know what's going on in the Realm, to be honest.

Veronica continues, "So, if it's Sol painting that mural, then why would it be of—"

"*A holiday portrait of Echo City.* Okay," I say with a jolt of excitement. "I think I'm following you now."

"This is the part where I say I'm not following at all. But one of you would have to actually care about that, so . . ."

"Sorry, Too Tall, this one's sorta hard to explain," I say. "But I think what Veronica's thinking is that Sol only paints murals *of the Realm.* So if he's painting a mural of the holidays in Echo City, which is right now, that might mean that right now, we're in the Realm."

"Right. Knew you'd catch on," says Veronica, marching down the stoop.

"King," says Tall, "I really appreciate you explaining all that to me. Now, I just gotta say, none of that makes any sense at all. And I'm worried about you."

"Come check out this mural with us. I'll explain on the way, okay?"

⚡

TOO TALL GETS the concept of the day on repeat as we turn left off Thurston Avenue. But he doesn't believe me that it's actually happening. How could he? He doesn't remember any of the previous trips we took through this same day.

Veronica sees the mural before I do. Her jaw clenches.

It must be a doozy.

I see the mural, and I get her reaction.

It's our street.

Ricks Street.

But it's lit up at night with all the thousands of Christmas lights that Crooked Eye painstakingly placed on the lamppost, the NO PARKING sign, the other NO PARKING sign, the phone lines, and even the fire hydrant; lights on the trees, around the windows, wires across the sidewalk, on the traffic lights—lit up as bright as a lightning strike. A Christmas supernova.

Only, Crooked Eye hasn't done all that.

Not yet.

"I don't believe it," I say.

V just shakes her head.

"What?" asks Tall. "What's the big deal?"

V turns to me. "This was here the whole time?"

"If Matteo saw it, I guess so," I say.

"Okay," V says, head in her hands. "This is hurting my brain."

"Nah, it's cool," says Tall. "I don't need to play in all your reindeer games."

"Tall, this mural? This hasn't happened yet. Remember, V and I have lived through today, Saturday, already. So we were both there when, later tonight, Crooked Eye puts all these lights up on Ricks Street. He lights it up and—"

"*Boom!*" Veronica shouts, startling him.

"Not funny," says Tall.

"Says you," says V.

"Uncle Crooked lights up the block, and then all the lights go out. Long Fingers's generator gets fried, and we go on a subway ride to the hardware store that stays open late."

"And then?"

"And then, it's yesterday, Friday night, and we're on the

41

way back from the Nets game to do it all over again," says Veronica.

"Messing with my head," I add.

"Wait—is *this* your phantom shoe pebble?" Tall asks.

I nod.

"Wow, dude, you have the weirdest problems." Too Tall folds his arms and examines the mural. "So this mural, it predicts the future?"

"Sorta," I say. "We're in a loop, Tall. So the future and the past, they're kinda the same thing."

"But why don't I remember any of this?" asks Tall. "According to you, I've been through it enough times."

"Don't feel bad," says Veronica. "I only just woke up myself. I didn't know what King was talking about, either, just two yesterdays ago."

"There's something about the routine of the day," I say. "It's like a lullaby—it hypnotizes you. Next thing you know, you're doing the same thing, acting the same way, and you can't help it. You know what's coming, but you react anyway. You forget you already did it till after you did it. It's like you've got amnesia, or you're dreaming."

"Or you're dreaming with amnesia?" Tall suggests. "So you're dreaming about your life, but you don't know it's yours?"

"Um, I guess?"

"But check out the mural style," says V. "It's definitely Sol."

I nod. "You can tell by the strong outlines and the intense colors, how's it all almost alive. And look!" I say, pointing to some silhouettes of people by one of the buildings beneath the lights. "That's us! Right? That's you, Tall!"

Too Tall peers closer, nodding. Then he steps back and examines the whole piece.

"What's that there?" he asks, pointing up at the starry backdrop of the mural.

V and I crook our heads back.

"What, the moon?" asks V.

"That's no moon," I say.

It's round and lit up bright, like the moon, but when we look more closely, we see a trail of light following after it. The rounded part shows a rocky surface surrounded by burning white fire. It feels like it's speeding toward us.

"Um, is that—" says Tall.

"A comet?" I say.

There's a moment of silence.

"We need to visit Sol," says V.

"Immediately," I agree.

WHEN WE GET to Cleopatra's Art Supplies, the doors are locked, and the storefront shutters are down. But that ribbed metal sheet is just another canvas for an artist like Sol. There's an amazing mural of ancient Egypt, of all things. There's the Sphinx, the pyramids behind it. Then there are these funny-headed gods. Some have animal heads, and others wear tall, fantastical headgear.

"They're really on the nose with this whole Cleopatra theme," says Veronica.

"Isis," says Tall, pointing to a woman wearing a cow-horned headdress. "Osiris." He points to a green man next to her. "Horus." He points to a falcon-headed figure. "Man,

I know this stuff cold. Wish Long Fingers could see me."

"Wonder why Sol is painting all these," I say. "I mean, if he's always painting what he sees in the Realm, how is he seeing all these Egyptian gods and things there?"

"Maybe he's just painting my homework," says Tall.

"Didn't you say Black Herman told you he visited echoes in ancient Egypt?" Veronica asks me.

"He sure did," I respond.

Black Herman is the greatest magician to ever live that most people have never heard of. Also, I met him. Even though he died in 1934. I met him in the Realm. Really cool guy.

"But where's the little guy?" says Tall.

We hear the *click-click-click* of the ball being shaken in a can of spray paint.

We follow the sound around the corner.

We find Sol spray-painting a mural on a half slab of Sheetrock. He's got one arm inside his coat, and the rest hangs off of him. The shirtsleeve on his other arm is rolled up so he can work the can.

Sula is standing behind him. She looks exhausted. Her arms are folded across her chest with a sherpa collar up high around her ears, trembling a little, like seeing her brother's one bare arm makes her extra cold.

"Oh, hey. Finally, you guys show," she says, unsurprised to see us.

"Y-you were expecting us?" I say.

"Well, yeah. I mean, I've been expecting someone to notice that time is standing still and we're living the same Friday and Saturday over and over."

Tall wrinkles his brow. "Are you guys on, like, a group chat I don't know about?"

"No," says Sula.

"How long have you known?" I ask.

"Hard to say. I only know, really, because of Sol."

"He *tells* you?" asks Veronica, surprised, since Sol never speaks.

"Trust me, Sol can get his point across when he wants to."

I turn to the muralist. I wonder if he's been aware of the time loop as long as I have, or longer. Has this been as hard for him as it has for me? Is he so ready for the day to do something different that he could scream?

Only, Sol is so wrapped up in the mural he's painting, he doesn't seem to notice me.

I wave a hand trying to get his attention. No luck.

"What's with him?" I whisper to Sula.

She shakes her head, and I notice that the bags under her eyes look like welts. "He's gone obsessed over painting. He just runs and runs like a little motor. He paints on everything, every surface he can. He painted every wall in the shop, stacks of paper; he barely eats or sleeps. I've just been trying to find him canvases and make sure he eats something. I don't know what else to do."

"What's that he's painting?" asks Veronica.

Against a dark backdrop is a strange symbol—a single arm running straight across, with a raised hand on each end that makes a sort of U shape.

"Somebody kick a field goal?" asks Too Tall.

He's right. It does look like the sign a football referee throws up for a field goal, arms out on each side and hands straight up, like goalposts.

"Only, the ref has a unibrow," I say, because of the way the single arm runs straight across.

"The ref *is* a unibrow," corrects Veronica.

"Think I seen it before, though," says Too Tall.

"That's the sign of Heka. The Egyptian god of magic," says Sula. "You know your Egyptian gods?"

"Not well enough, apparently," answers Tall.

"Don't feel bad," says Sula. "I only know because my dad was obsessed with the magicians of ancient Egypt. Heka doesn't get a lot of play, like Isis and Horus. But his name is also the ancient Egyptian word for magic, the magic that created and rules the cosmos."

"Sounds powerful," I say.

"You have no idea."

"The cosmos—like, stars and planets and stuff?" asks Tall.

"You know of some other cosmos?" snaps Sula.

"And comets and asteroids, I think he means," says Veronica.

"We noticed in one of Sol's murals—he painted the Christmas lights around my family's brownstone. There's this big object crashing down from the sky."

Sula turns and looks up to the sky. She squints in the December sun, and I notice her hair is starting to grow back in. I see that Sol, too, is growing some hair on his head. When we first met, they were both bald. We found out that Sol's hair stopped growing because Urma was draining his life-energy. Sula shaved her own head every day out of solidarity. Is Sol's hair growing now that his vampiric Realm-lady mom is gone?

"It's there," she says, pointing. "It doesn't look like anything. But it's coming."

I look up to where she points. I see a speck, but it could be a plane or a helicopter, as far as I can tell.

"Let's take this inside," says Sula. "There's something I need to show you."

SULA WASN'T KIDDING about Sol's painting. Every imaginable surface is exploding with restless color and images. A lot of the paintings are of ancient Egypt, but not all. There are also scenes from Echo City, even one of us riding the subway. There are scenes from backyards in the countryside, and from ancient cities with folks dressed up like a costume drama in the movies. There are castles and architecture from all over the world. A lot of it is really beautiful. It must be so strange to be Sol and see this stuff in your head all the time. At first it sounded cool to me, like he would have some adventure every time he closed his eyes. But there are *so many* of them, it's disturbing. Like Sol is being attacked by these visions, almost. Does he ever want some peace and quiet?

Just to get Sol to come inside, Sula gives him a fresh sketchbook and a set of pencils. Sol is quickly off and doodling, holding one pencil between his forefinger and thumb, and another three wedged between his knuckles on standby.

Sula leads us through a painting-covered hallway to a painting-covered door and opens it to reveal . . .

The bathroom.

"Sorry to bring you back here. But it's where I saw this," says Sula.

She pulls away the shower curtain. I almost choke as I see a well-known face painted on the tile wall.

It's *my dad*.

He looks aged, his beard grown, with more salt in his pepper. Not like one of Mom's photos of him as a young man, but rather what he should look like now. Close to how he was when I saw him and almost had him back this past summer.

He has a box in his hands—the Magician's Lost and Found. It's the box I found beneath the stage of the Mercury Theater. The box where I lost my hand, which opened up the magic of the Realm to me.

Pops is placing something inside. It's a brassy gold triangle made of some kind of metal with a jewel at its center, and it has a chain attached to it.

"*Dad.*"

"This is the other reason I was expecting you to show," says Sula.

I peer closer at the picture, hovering over the bathtub. "What is that he's placing in there?"

The triangle explodes with light and color. Seems like it took a lot of paint to make that effect. I've seen something like it before, but I can't place it.

"It's some kind of stone," says Sula.

"Is he trying to pass that back to us?" I wonder. "Man, I wish we still had the Magician's Lost and Found." I lost it when I had to send it through the Mirror to close the portal to the Realm.

Sula then lowers her head and removes a chain from around her neck. As she draws it up, she reveals that beneath her T-shirt is the same pyramid-shaped stone in the picture.

It dangles there in front of my eyes, twirling on its chain like a dreidel.

"Way ahead of you," says Sula.

⚡

WE'RE IN SULA and Sol's storeroom, sitting on empty, upside-down plaster buckets. I have the pyramid-shaped thing in my hands and am caressing each line of this strange stone. I understand the effect Sol was going for with his painting in the bathroom. The stone itself captures a bunch of reflections all at once. A smooth, perfect circle is carved dead center of the stone.

My face appears, filling the shape of the circle. But it's not like a normal mirror, more like my reflection was summoned there somehow, and as I move my head around, the reflection lags a moment or two.

"King?"

"King?"

"King!"

V's hand moves in front of the stone and snaps me out of it.

"Sorry!" I say. It's like when I look at this stone, there's a gap between me and the world around me.

"Sula is trying to show you something," says V, looking at me like I've got six heads.

And that's kinda how I feel . . .

Sula is holding out a box.

I think it's the Magician's Lost and Found at first, but

then I realize there's all these ancient Egyptian etchings on it.

"Whoa," I say. "Where'd you get this, now?"

"Found it with my dad's old things," she says.

There are four symbols carved in the wood, one on each side. One image is of a solar disk between two horns, like Tall said belongs to Isis. Beneath that is a carving of a falcon head. There's some sort of jackal head on another side, and then the last picture is of a miniature green guy with his arms crossed over his chest, like a sarcophagus.

Tall points to each symbol. "Isis, Horus, Set, and Osiris. Four Egyptian gods."

"Like Illusion, Mystic, Force, and Sorcery. The four elements of magic on my old box."

"That's because it's the same thing," says Sula.

"What do you mean?"

"My dad left behind a whole room full of *curiosities*, as he called them. When I saw that mural on the bathroom wall, it got me thinking about your box, and how you said stuff was passed through from the Realm. So I went and checked this box, and it was *glowing blue*. Like, Realm-portal blue. I open it, and there's this pyramid-stone-looking thing."

"It's wild," I say, holding the stone up like a pocket mirror. A warm thrill charges through my Realm hand. I wait for the center sphere to catch my reflection again. It takes a second. But soon enough, my face emerges from the depths of the heart of the stone. "So it's like a mirror, almost? What's it made of?"

"No idea," says Sula. "I try not to look at it too much—you get lost. My dad had one just like it. Maybe it's the same one? All I know is I hate that thing. Ever since it came, my brother's been tormented by all these images."

"Your dad had one of these triangle stone things?" I ask.

"Yeah. Only he kept it pretty well hidden. I'd catch him sometimes, staring into it late at night. The more I'd see him with it, the wilder the stuff he'd start talking about the Realm."

"Like what kinda wild stuff?" I ask warily.

Sula rubs her temples like the memory causes a massive headache. "Oh, just your typical squirrel's stash of nuts."

"Like?" I ask.

Too Tall and Veronica seem to hold their breaths as they scoot their buckets closer to Sula.

"Like resetting the timeline, ending life as we know it, and smashing today's reality with a comet."

My entire brain screeches like a record scratch.

"Say what now?"

"She's kidding," says Tall. "Isn't she?"

Sula shrugs, like, believe whatever you like.

"I don't think she's kidding," says V.

"I need this way, way slower, please," I say. "These words you're saying, they sound absurd."

"I forgot your dad, like, protected you from this kind of stuff. Do you know about the alpha?"

I shake my head. "Should I?"

She sighs, like this is going to take more out of her than she's got right now.

"So you don't even know how the Realm was made?"

I shake my head. "I never really thought about it. Always assumed it was just there."

"Everything starts somewhere. There's always a beginning. Even the universe has to begin," says Sula.

"Sure," Too Tall pops in. "Big-bang style."

"Right, well, there was a sort of *bang* that created the Realm," says Sula. "About twelve thousand years ago, a comet hit our planet."

"Hmm," says Veronica, "must have skipped that in history class."

Tall nods. "Mr. Cruikshank never mentioned that."

"I bet Mr. Cruikshank never traveled to a twelve-thousand-year-old echo and saw the comet, either," says Sula.

"True story," says Tall.

"Wait, you went into the Realm?" I ask.

"No. But my dad went back to the alpha, the very first echo and the beginning of the Realm, when the comet hit twelve thousand years ago."

"Wait, that doesn't make sense," I say. I think about the apparently infinite chain of echoes I saw when I was in the Realm. "How could he go back that far? You can't jump through that many echoes. There have to be thousands."

Sula's eyes fall on the stone in my gloved hand. "Well, Dad did it somehow. Came back and said a comet hit us, and it was so big it decimated most life on the planet. He said modern science has no clue it even happened."

"You'd think they could figure out something like that," says V.

"Quackademics don't know a solar disk from a Frisbee." Tall does his best gruff Uncle Long Fingers impression.

Veronica turns to him. "You sound way too much like my father."

"Sorry. Been listening to him so much. I hear his voice when I go to sleep at night."

"I'm sorry," says V as she pats his knee.

"So, if the planet got hit by a comet, why don't we know about it?" I ask Sula.

"I'm not a scientist. But it's true. I mean, it makes sense. Our planet—us—we're out here in a shooting gallery of a solar system, just sorta hanging like a target, while these space particles the size of Brooklyn whizz by. You think we're not gonna get hit? Well, we did. A comet hit us so hard and so fast, it had to create an extra dimension just for all that kinetic energy. That's the Realm. Another plane of existence."

"Okay, I think I follow you. So that's why Sol painted the comet in that mural of the Christmas lights on Ricks

Street?" I say. "Because it's the comet from twelve thousand years ago?"

"Well, yes and no."

"I like the 'yes' part. Not so much the 'no' part," I say.

Sula stands up and paces. She scratches her elbows as she talks, like a nervous tic. "Dad always said, to reset the Realm, you have to go to the alpha. The beginning."

"Um, *reset* the Realm?" I repeat. "What does that mean, exactly? Why would one do that?"

"The Realm is full of all these echoes, right? Twenty-six-hour loops of time, perfectly preserved. Well, what if you wanted to make one of *those* echoes keep going?"

"Keep going, like, past hour twenty-six?" I say.

"Yeah, just make time keep marching forward," says Sula. "That's what Dad would mean when he'd talk about resetting the Realm."

"Well, that doesn't sound too terrible, unless something then has to happen to *our* time."

"Kingston, there can only be *one primary timeline*." I get a weird chill when she says my name like that. It makes me sound more important than I'm used to—like she really needs my help. "Listen, I don't know how he did it. But somehow, my dad made our world, our timeline *now*, the one to get hit by the comet. He's gone into the Realm, and he's going to make some other timeline the timeline that keeps going forward. When he does that, the comet will wipe us out completely."

"You're saying your dad is going to—*swap* cosmos between *ours* and some point in the past that got demolished by a comet?"

"You actually caught on pretty quick."

"I mean, I thought I must have just misheard you somehow."

"Don't I wish. But no. I never would have believed it if we hadn't entered this loop. If I hadn't seen my brother paint that comet in the sky."

"But that's so . . . *evil*," I say.

"Don't look at me. I told you my dad was up to no good. Why do you think I never wanted to go get him back from the Realm when you were desperate to get yours? I thought he was better off in the Realm. I thought we were all better off. Boy, was I wrong."

"But wouldn't he care about you? And Sol? Wouldn't that stop him?"

"Listen, that man can be very self-righteous when he wants to. He can justify almost *anything*. He probably worked it out that it's for the greater good somehow, I don't know. To him, it would be like none of us ever existed."

"This is the wildest thing I've ever heard," says V.

"My dad would always talk about it," Sula explains. "How he was born out of sync with time and belonged to another era, a time gone by where he's not some second-rate magician in Preston James's shadow," she says with a bite at the end.

I never quite thought of Maestro that way, as *in my father's shadow*, but the bitterness in her tone comes from someplace real.

"You make it sound like he's doing all this to chase my father somehow," I say.

"I think he was—*is*. We haven't seen my dad for years, but he's very much alive and very much messing with our reality. And this obsession with the Realm—all that started with your dad, somehow."

"What makes you say that?"

"Just trust me, okay?" she says, getting impatient. "Your dad has always been around my family like some kinda ghost. Now he's, like, literally on my bathroom wall. He passed that device back to you. I think he needs your help. I think you need to go."

"Are you asking me to leave?"

"No, I mean *go into the Realm*," Sula enunciates.

Once she says it loud and clear, I realize I knew all

along what she meant. I've known since I saw Pop in that mural. Maybe I've known since the whole déjà vu thing started that I'd have to go back. That I wasn't finished with the Realm, or the Realm wasn't finished with me.

"And this pyramid-looking thing? You think this is important?" I ask.

"It's something. So you know how the echo resets to four in the evening each time?" Sula says, pointing to a clock on the wall. "Well, I wore this around my neck, and when the echo reset? It was still around my neck."

"Wait, you mean—" Veronica jumps in, staring down at the stone like it just got a thousand times more important.

"Yup. It breaks the rules. It's some kinda magic. Everything else about reality resets completely, except this. I was out back, rummaging for stuff for Sol to paint. Next thing I know, it's the day before, I'm ringing up a customer at the store for a set of watercolors. And the stone is still around my neck. 'Huh,' the customer says, 'that's pretty,' with this weird look like she was surprised she'd never noticed it before."

"Because it wasn't there before," says Veronica.

"Bingo. And ever since I've had it on, I've been totally aware every time the echo resets. I remember everything," says Sula.

"Me too," says V. "But I'm not wearing an ancient stone or hiding an invisible hand."

Sula locks eyes with V.

"Well, that just means whatever is special about you is still a mystery," Sula tells her.

I catch Sol peeking over his shoulder at V. She looks back, almost like they're communicating. V stares down at him and then looks up through the skylight.

It's a weird moment, but I get distracted from my thought as Sula dangles the stone in front of me like a hypnotic watch.

"I think you're going to need this more than me," Sula says.

"You're just giving it to me?" I ask.

She nods. "I need to get it away from Sol. I feel like it's infecting his brain somehow. When I first found it, Sol put it around his neck. Next thing I know, he can't stop painting Realm images. So I took it from him. I catch him looking for it from time to time, even when it's under my shirt, out of sight."

"Your dad sent it here for a reason," says Tall. "For you, King—right?"

"Last he knew, you had the Magician's Lost and Found," says V. "He probably thinks you still have it."

I place the chain around my neck, feeling the stone warm against my chest. "What am I supposed to do with it, though?"

"I know my dad is able to choose what echo he goes to in the Realm somehow. That's how he got back to the alpha. Maybe that's it?"

Sol tugs on my sleeve. I'm so fixed on the stone and Sula, I forgot he was there, sketching on his pad. He hands it to me.

There's a drawing of the stone, perfect right down to the detail, even the size. The only difference is the center of the triangle isn't just a blank circle.

Instead, there's the Watch of 13, set neatly in place like a puzzle piece.

I KNOW OF two Watches of 13 in this world. There's the one that was lodged in the Magician's Lost and Found. I don't have that one anymore, since it was *in* the box when I used it as a wrecking ball to destroy Maestro's Mirror.

The other Watch of 13 is in Uncle Long Fingers's workshop.

We say goodbye to Sula and Sol. I wish we could hang out more. I wish they could come with us, even. But Sula has her hands full trying to take care of Sol. He'll barely eat without her help.

The sun is bright out on the street, and the chill hits my face like an open-handed slap. I pop the faux-fur-trimmed hoodie up from my coat.

"*Brrr*," says Tall, hands disappearing inside the sleeves of his bubble coat. "It got brick out here."

"Or Sula's story chilled you to the bone," says V.

"Every time I come out of that shop, the world feels different," says Tall. "I mean, you guys buying any of that stuff?"

"Are you really doubting it?" asks V.

"She's been pretty on point in the past, Tall," I say.

"Well, I guess I don't understand something. Are we in the Realm, like, now?" asks Tall.

"Maestro made our timeline into an echo. That's why we're living in a loop. He wants to make some other point in history the new prime reality. And once he does that, this comet is going to hit us. Unless we stop him. Make sense?"

"When you put it like that, yes," says Tall. "Now, how do we do that?"

Sula made it sound simple. *You've got to go,* she said. Only she doesn't know how to do it, either.

Go back to the Realm. Find Dad.

But how?

I shrug and glance over to Veronica. She looks as clueless as I feel.

"We need my dad's watch," she says, recovering. "For that stone thingy."

"I was thinking the same thing," I say, nodding energetically. "But he's got it in his workshop, and he, like, never leaves."

"We need to distract Long Fingers?" says Tall with a wink and a smirk. "I got you."

⚡

Too Tall is deep into Operation Mass Distraction—as Tall calls the scheme to distract Long Fingers—so I can sneak in and grab his Watch of 13. I have to admit, his acting skills are on point. He asks Long Fingers to explain something about Egyptian astrology. "The Egyptian astrological principle—how do you say it, Uncle Long? *As above . . . so go?*"

"As above, so below," Long Fingers snaps at Tall like a catfish on the bait.

Tall keeps playing dense and asks him to show him up on the roof with the real stars. My uncle gives Tall a side-eye that's sharp as an elbow, but then he sighs and takes him upstairs.

Veronica and I go to Long Fingers's bookcase, where old books of magic and grimoires are lined from wall to wall and floor to ceiling. I reach right for the spine of the book *The Four Elements of Magic*—by now, I know the location on the shelf by heart. I tilt the book toward me and feel the wall mechanism catch and the bookcase groan and move in its grooves. I step through the opening.

The foyer's four walls are dedicated to the four elements of magic. Each wall has photos of a famous magic trick that embodies one of those elements. Hooker's Vanishing Deck for Illusion. The Skull of Balsamo for Mystic. William Tell's Pistol for Force, and Maestro's Mirror for Sorcery. Above the hallway to Long Fingers's workshop, there's a legend: THE FOUR ELEMENTS OPEN THE WAY.

I learned this past summer that the phrase isn't just about using the book *The Four Elements of Magic* to open the bookcase. It's also about opening an *actual* way—as in portal—to the Realm. When you bring all four elemental tricks close together, that opens a portal to the Realm. Veronica and Too Tall helped me figure it out.

Three of the elements—my dad's old tricks—I last saw on the stage of the Mercury Theater. Could they still be there, stuck in the crystal? Or did that federal Omega team remove them?

And even if the three tricks are there, we don't have the Mirror. What do we do about the fourth element, Sorcery?

Only thing I know for sure is that I need the Watch of 13. Maybe when I set the watch in the "pyramid thingy," as V calls it, I'll get some answers.

I hope.

Long Fingers's lab is as chaotic as ever, a sprawl of sketches and mechanical doohickeys that probably only make sense to one single man on this earth. I see something new on the shelf. It's an ancient Egyptian statue, of all things. It's solid black stone. Seems like Egypt is everywhere these days.

I circle the drafting table. It looks small and lonely without the great bearded one behind it. Glancing up, I see the plaque where he hangs the Watch of 13, only—

There's no watch.

"Think your uncle don't know what time it is?"

My heart jumps, and I spin my head around before my body can catch up.

There's Long Fingers holding the Watch of 13 by its chain.

"H-HEY, UNC, FUNNY seeing you here," I blurt out.

"Funny? Is that right? Funny like strange, or funny like ha-ha funny?" he asks.

"Neither, I guess. I don't know why I said that," I say, my cheeks hot with embarrassment.

"Since this is my lab, my question would then be, why *wouldn't* I be here? Is it 'cause of your over-tall friend's song and dance 'bout getting me up on the roof?" His glare burns into me. "Did you really expect me to fall for that?"

I lower my head. I can't even make eye contact anymore.

"Don't answer that. I know you did. I need you to tell me why."

I don't waste any time trying to come up with stories

or excuses. I explain about the loop, and the mural with the comet, Sula's story, Dad painted on the bathroom wall, and the stone thingy passed from the Realm.

As I talk, I wonder, did Long Fingers know to take the watch with him somehow? It's not like he ever walks around with it, as far as I know. But right when I needed it, he took it.

He sits down behind his table and blinks his watery eyes like a very large toad on a log. "And you didn't think to come to me with this?" he asks.

"I'm sorry, Uncle. I thought—I was afraid—"

"That I'd stop you," he says. "I get it. And ordinarily, I would."

I pause on the word. *"Ordinarily?"* I repeat.

"Ordinarily," he says, nodding. "But nothing is ordinary. Not now. It only feels that way."

"Wait—what do you mean?"

"When you get to my age, it's hard to tell sometimes. Lotta days feel like a loop. Like, just wind us up, let us go, and we do the same things in the same spaces and can't barely tell the difference between Tuesday and Wednesday anyway."

"You okay, Unc?" I ask.

"I'm *old*," he says. "Too old." He holds out a hand with those famous fingers. "Let me see it." More demand than request, reminding me of when I showed him my invisible hand this past summer.

I take the stone from around my neck.

He examines it with awe, staring into the center circle until, after a long moment, Long Fingers's face fills the triangle like light through a prism. "The Echo Stone. Pure magical genius in a triangle. Proportional perfection. Crafted from the rock that made the Realm itself. Twelve thousand years ago," he says, nodding.

"When you look at it, it takes a sec before your reflection shows. Why is that?" I ask.

"What do you think it's doing?" he asks me instead.

"Honestly, when it pauses, it's almost like it *chooses* what to reflect, somehow. Does that make sense?"

He throws me a knowing side-eye. "Very astute. This object has *agency*."

"What's that mean?"

"It has a will of its own."

"Like, it makes decisions?"

"Now, I didn't say it has *consciousness*. That's different. Consciousness implies thought. No, this merely has a will. It is an entity of power, and it must be mastered."

He cups the stone in both hands and gazes dead center. His reflection repeats as if within the boxes of a 3-D grid. Then the image flickers and changes. New faces and shapes manifest one after the other. It's like I'm seeing his every thought expressed as a picture. James family members, old and young, past and present, laughing, crying; oddball objects being assembled beneath his expert hands; our brownstone front doors looming devilish and terrifying . . . These images and more blur by in this dreamlike way. I can barely register what they are before they're gone, and then I can hardly recall what I think I saw. It's like seeing into a person's mind that's so full of references and shorthand that it really doesn't make any sense, unless you actually are the person.

And strangely, I think I see . . . *Egypt*.

Then a single object fills the intricate stone. It's the black Egyptian statue that I noticed earlier, smooth carved and facing forward with calm, knowing eyes.

Then I see Long Fingers isn't looking at the stone anymore. He's locked eyes with the statue on the shelf. The stone, as though projecting his mind, shows what he is looking at.

"What do you see when you look at this statue?" Long Fingers asks.

"What? The Egyptian dude?" I say.

"Dude?" he repeats. "Or king?"

"King, I guess?"

"Good guess. You know he's a king 'cause of the head-dress. And the skinny chin-beard," he says, combing fingers through his own thicket of beard hair. "But get closer. Tell me what you see."

The Egyptian king faces me head-on. He's well built and very stiff. His headdress comes down at an angle on either side, so he looks like a triangle with an invisible point above the center of his head. He's got broad shoulders, and his arms rest neatly on his knees. The statue is so straight from shoulders to toes, I only realize he's seated when I look from an angle. He sits on a throne.

"He's a king," I say. "He's on a throne. And there's a cobra on his headdress."

"The uraeus," says Long Fingers. "Another sign of his office. Means he's a king. Does that make him important?"

"I guess so."

"What else do you see?"

I come up along its side, so the statue is almost in profile. I take a sharp breath as I realize something is on his head. A bird is attached to the back of the headdress.

"A bird?" I say.

"A falcon," says Long Fingers.

The falcon is perched on the top of the throne with

wings aligned with the angle of the king's headdress so it connects at the tips of the wing feathers. The bird's eyes gaze out from just above the king's head.

"It's strange. You can't see the bird at all when you look head-on. But from the side, it appears like the falcon is taller than the king. Like he sees more."

"*Yes.* The falcon is invisible. Yet the falcon is higher than the mind of the king. The falcon is a *higher consciousness*."

"Okay . . ."

"Remember this about the ancient Egyptians. Nothing is by chance. They make no mistakes. They are extremely symbolic."

"They *are*?"

"Are, were, what's the difference?"

"Um, isn't there a big difference?" I ask.

"We're all echoes now, Kingston, unless things get set right. Ancient Egypt? Just a jump away."

"Wait, are you saying—"

"I'm saying exactly what I'm saying. I need you to pay attention and listen to me. You're going to need to understand what I'm telling you very soon."

I swallow my next words. *He knows I'm going to the Realm,* I realize. *He's sending me there.*

"Now look at the statue again. See the falcon? That's

the god Horus. The king's god, the god of the pharaohs. And the king's higher consciousness."

"Um, Uncle? I don't really understand. What do you mean by *higher consciousness*?"

"King, you know how sometimes, when you focus, you can do amazing things with your Realm hand?" he asks.

"Yeah?"

"And sometimes, you can't? Sometimes, when you reach for a saltshaker, it won't even budge for you? I've seen you try. See, your *higher self* is in touch with your creativity and all that power. When that's realized, you can *astonish*, Kingston."

"My higher self," I repeat without meaning to. My ears tingle, and I wave my hand as if there's an invisible bird of prey back there.

Long Fingers closes his eyes as though he's concentrating on the Echo Stone in his hands. After a moment, the image of the pharaoh vanishes.

He opens his eyes and hands the Echo Stone back to me, now with the appearance of an innocent, triangular pendant of costume jewelry.

"See, a magician can master this stone like how the falcon masters the king. The stone has no consciousness. So it reaches into your mind to fill the stone. You know how the

Realm needs reality so it has something to copy, to make an echo? You're right that it doesn't reflect what's around it. Not physically, anyway. It reflects what you're *thinking*."

"So when I saw my own face . . ."

"You were thinking about yourself."

"Oh."

"Don't be ashamed, it's only natural. You expected to see yourself, so you did. Just be warned—sharing mind space with the stone is treacherous. When a magician merges his own consciousness with the stone's power, he *might* be able to see all the echoes to ever exist the way you might, I don't know, remember what you had for breakfast this morning. That magician would be a sort-of master of the Realm. He or she could travel to any echo, just by thinking it when stepping through the portal. But you have to know your limits. The stone is still an entity of the Realm, and the Realm is too enormous, too cosmic for any one individual. Trying to get your mind around all of it could drive a magician down a dangerous path."

"Like Maestro," I say. "Sula said her dad got to a point where she didn't even recognize him when he had that thing. And Sol. It's like he sees the Realm, all of it, all the time, and can't get away, so he paints."

My uncle nods gravely. I stare into the Echo Stone

with a sinking terror in my gut. I suddenly feel like I'm holding the whole universe in my hand. The image of my face appears in the stone.

Then Uncle Long takes the Watch of 13 and sets it inside the center circle. The watch lands with a *click*, almost like it's magnetized. As soon as it does, my reflection vanishes.

"I invented this watch as a kind of shortcut to mastering the stone. See, it blocks the center from fixing on your mind, and the clock mechanism makes it so you can set any echo you wish to travel to." He grins with a hint of pride.

"Wow, Unc, that's genius."

"Now come up on the roof. Let's see what starlight does to it."

VERONICA IS SITTING on the couch by the bookcase, tapping her fingers nervously.

When she sees me, she hops to her feet and holds up her hands. "King, I know I said I was gonna be your lookout. But Dad had the watch, and said he had to talk to you—"

"It's okay, V," I say.

"You don't need to apologize to him," Long Fingers makes clear to her. "That fool boy tried to deceive me and steal from me. If it weren't for the circumstances, his hide would be mine."

"Circumstances? What circumstances?" she asks.

"Follow me," he says, marching for the staircase.

"What? So you can tell King, but not me?"

Long Fingers turns around slowly. "I'm 'bout to *show* both of you."

Watching Long Fingers take the old brownstone stairs all the way up to the roof is like witnessing a lone man walk a rickety bridge above a tempest. There's swaying and groaning and pauses for breath and holding on for dear life.

Out on the roof, our breaths appear and disappear in front of us. Too Tall is standing in the center of the roof, holding his hands up with his thumbs and forefingers touching like the delta sign to the sky. We've barely got our coats on, just zipping up as the cold attacks our bones. The Brooklyn streets lurk below, and the stars feel that much closer.

"You got it?" calls Long Fingers.

"I think I got it," says Too Tall. "Really hard to see, though."

"Light pollution," Long Fingers says to us. "Once the blackout hits, you'll see it."

"What's he doing?" asks V.

"Tall, what are you doing?" I ask.

"Trapping Orion's Belt in my hands triangle," Tall says like that's obvious.

"Your 'hands triangle'?" I repeat.

"Yeah, sorry, King. Operation Mass Distraction was a straight failure. When we got up here, he told me to do this and went down to get you."

Long Fingers gets behind Too Tall and looks up through the gap in his hands at the night sky. "Looks good," he says with one eye closed.

"Thanks, Uncle Long, but why am I doing this exactly?" asks Too Tall.

"What'd I tell you about asking questions?"

"You told me to always question everything," says Tall.

"Oh," my uncle says like he wasn't quite expecting that. "Well, yes, I guess that sounds like something I'd say."

Uncle Long takes the Echo Stone and hands it to Tall.

"Now hold this exactly where your hands were. Faceup, so the watch sees the sky."

Too Tall does as he's told and holds the stone up to the stars.

"Okay, we just need a blackout and—"

As he speaks, the blackout that canceled Crooked Eye's light show rolls over Echo City. Lampposts, streetlights, and holiday twinkles are extinguished like candles. All I see is dark, rectangular roofs spread beneath the towering Black Rock of BK. It hulks above the city with its dark outline against the night sky. Purple seethes from within like embers of burning coal.

"Huh," says Long Fingers, looking at the stone. "It's not working. Should light up like the heavens, this thing."

"What? Am I doing it wrong?" says Tall.

"You got Orion's Belt?" asks Long Fingers.

"Yeah, I think so!"

"Let me see," says my uncle. He takes the device in his hands and turns it this way and that like a steering wheel to the sky. "I mean, the cosmos doesn't just flip on its axis. It takes thousands of years for the stars to move that much."

"Pops, what's going on?" Veronica asks.

He takes ahold of Veronica's shoulder. "You're going to need to get your cousin to the other tricks—the Skull, the Pistol, and the Deck. Once you awaken the stone by starlight, the way should reopen. If a gate opens in one spot more than once, it's easier to open another gate. The veil between our worlds is thinnest there."

"Dad," she says. "Are you sending us to the Realm?"

"You won't have much time." He shows her the Watch of 13 now lodged in the stone. "The big hand tells you what time it is here, your home time. The little hand sets where you're going." He turns the little hand all the way to the top, a hair after the 13.

"*Where?*" says V. "*When?*"

"The beginning, of course. That's the only place the stone can reset the world to rights."

"The . . . *alpha*?" she says.

Her dad nods. "You got it. You'll figure it out. You're the smartest one. Smarter than me. And you're more special than you think."

"Why would you say that? You've never said anything like that to me," V says. I can't tell if she's upset or touched by her dad's words.

"Because I know these things, and now you need to know them as well," says Long Fingers. "There's only one smarter than us all, and if you meet her, say hi. You'll know when it's her."

"Okay, Pop, are you just trying to mess with my head? 'Cause I'm feeling all kinds of ways about what you're saying right now."

"Unc," I say. Ordinarily, we'd be volunteering for a subway ride around now. We're getting dangerously close to the end of the loop. "I think we've got to hurry."

"You're catching on," my uncle says with a smirk.

There's a rumble, like a fleet of eighteen-wheelers passing on the streets below.

"What is that?" V looks at me.

The buildings shake.

"Um, I thought we didn't get earthquakes," says Too Tall.

"It's here," says Long Fingers.

"What's here?" I say.

I'm thinking, *I can't be surprised. I've been through this day too many times. I know it all, like clockwork. The blackout. The train ride. The reset.*

The rumble of the train . . .

A light grows on the horizon, like a rising purple sun. It's the Black Rock of BK, and it's lit up like someone flipped a bulb on inside.

I see V mouth the words, *Look up.* The rumble is so loud, I can barely hear.

She mouths the words again, *Look up.* It's like she's said them before, but this version of tonight, I've never been here before. Has V?

The stars in the sky are falling in every direction.

"I don't think those are shooting stars," shouts V, walking closer to the edge of the rooftop.

She's right. The streaks aren't going across the sky—they are coming right toward us.

Blazing globes that turn from white streaks to red-hot boulders in the sky. Hundreds of them fall like hail.

"The One. The alpha," says Long Fingers in awe, looking at the sky. He brings the Echo Stone over to me and places the chain around my neck. The triangle shape rests against my chest. "Careful with that thing. There's an absurd amount of magic in there. The wrong sort of tremor could shatter it, and you don't want to be anywhere near that thing if it breaks."

"Okay," I say.

His face tilts toward the sky like a prayer to the heavens. "The Word. In the beginning was the Word . . . I am that which created the Word . . . I am the Word . . . I am the Eternal . . ."

"All righty," says Tall, "he's lost it."

I feel the heat at my back. The light is screaming bright, and my shadow falls long over my cousin.

V holds her hand up like she's pointing.

I turn. A ball of fire is just a few seconds from turning us all to dust.

"Everyone, get down!" she shouts.

Her fingers are outstretched to the sky.

A rock glowing like it was spewed out of a volcano just stops midair. Rotating like time itself has stopped.

"V, are you—how'd you—?"

Know to do that?

V looks like she can hardly believe it herself. "King, I—It's like I've been here before. I knew what to do. Sol, at Cleopatra's, he was talking to me. He told me, 'Look up.'"

"He doesn't talk," Tall shouts back.

"I know," she says.

Her words are swallowed by the rumble of the falling stars.

She holds a boulder-sized rock that glows as red as Crooked Eye's Christmas lights above all of us.

The sky is lit up with thousands of fireballs. More than V or I or anyone could ever stop. But she stopped this one.

The falling sky roars in my ears. I close my eyes.

The roar becomes a rumble.

Thum-da-doom. Thum-da-doom.

V AND I are still holding eye contact as the subway rumbles through the tunnels.

Crooked Eye snores as my cousin and I have a whole conversation without words.

Did you really stop that boulder?

I think I really stopped that boulder.

But it's coming back.

It's going to destroy us.

Unless . . .

Unless we do something about it.

Unless we stop him.

How?

We have to go.

Where?

"The Realm," I say out loud.

It's the only word that had to be said.

V nods to something by my chest.

I look down.

It's the brassy-gold Echo Stone, still around my neck where Uncle Long Fingers placed it, with the Watch of 13 lodged in its center, both hands set to the 13. I see the big hand has moved slightly right. "It's starting," I say, and I tuck it under my hoodie and zip up.

The train slows. The snoring stops.

"Let's go, sleepyfaces. It's our stop."

We step out onto the platform. V and I hang back.

"Okay. What's the move?" I say.

"The Mercury," she says, but I knew she'd say that. "There've been a couple portals there, so let's make it one more."

"What about Too Tall?" I ask.

"What about him?"

"He . . . We need him, don't we?"

"*Need* him?" V snaps. "Why, lose your stepladder?"

"He knows things," I say.

"Does he? He's at the beginning of the loop. He won't know anything that happened—not Sula's, not the roof, nothing."

"It doesn't matter. He doesn't need to know why. If we need him, he'll come. That's how he is. That's why we need him."

V shrugs. "If you say so," she says doubtfully.

"Watch. *Tall*," I shout as he walks ahead of us, zoning out at the platform posters. I wave him back to me while Crooked Eye keeps on walking to the turnstile. "We've got to go back to the Realm. Like, ASAP."

He screws his face all the way up. *"What?"*

"Shh, we don't want Uncle Crooked to hear," says V.

Tall realizes that if V is saying this, it must be true. His eyes bug out, and he takes in a huge breath, like he's going to either shout or sneeze. I don't give him the chance. I jump and cover his mouth.

"Please, Tall," I say slowly, "just listen. Time is trapped in an echo. Maestro is trying to eliminate our timeline. We have to reset time back to normal. Are you coming?" I let go of his mouth.

"Am I—*what*? What are y—"

"Tall, I need to know right now."

"Am I *coming*? Of course I'm coming. You'll explain

along the way, though? I prefer it when I can follow along."

I turn to Veronica. "See?"

⚡

WE REACH THE street in time for the first blackout. The Black Rock of BK looms above Echo City like a grim reminder of where we have to go.

The city lights flicker back on. Usually, Too Tall makes a comment about those outages being "a trip, boy," but he's quiet now. I guess he's still thinking about what I told him and where we're going.

Last time around, Veronica got rid of Crooked Eye by talking like on fast-forward, but now she's quiet, too.

"You kids want some dinner?" Crooked breaks the silence. "Pizza? It's your world."

"Wow, what a crazy blackout, huh?" V says. She's repeating what she said before, but her timing is off. "So dark! Say, Unc, we were thinking us kids might go meet some friends, you cool if we meet up back at the house later tonight? Um, how 'bout that?"

Same idea, wrong tone. Last time, Crooked had no chance. But now she sounds unsure of herself. He suspects something.

"Wh-why would . . ." He loses his question as he seems to think of something. "Hey," he says, a smile brightening his face, "I get it, kids got to do what kids got to do."

He reaches into his pockets, rummaging for something. Veronica almost looks guilty.

He pulls out a small change pouch and hands it to me.

"Take this, just in case you kids need something to eat or run into any problems," he says with a wink. He bows and strolls away, whistling in the evening.

I take a peek inside the small pouch. A random assortment of coins from who-knows-where that no right-minded Brooklynite would accept.

Does Crooked know more than he lets on? I wonder as we close in on the Mercury.

I get this nervous feeling in my belly. Last time I went to the Realm, I didn't plan on it. It was an instant decision— I jumped into the portal to get away from something worse. Now that I'm actually planning to go, I think of the Echo Stone and imagine all the terrible spots I might wind up in. I think of Sol's murals plastered all over their store and warehouse like I'm on a nightmare tour of all those far-out places.

Seeing the tents stops me cold.

Blue pop-up tents make a perimeter around the crystal base of the theater.

I forgot. The Omega team.

V, Tall, and I huddle up.

"Forgot about those guys," says V.

"Me too," I say. "Think anybody's still there?"

"I see shadows," says Tall, his neck craning. "There are definitely people in that big tent there."

"We need another way in," says V.

"Check. We know of two. There's the chute by the wall—"

"BRICK WALL!" Tall whisper-shouts, and he flashes up his flat hands. "Come on," he says, chuckling. "Just trying to lighten the mood."

"—and the sewers," V continues, ignoring Tall.

I lead the way across the street to the manhole where we once escaped the Mercury Theater this summer.

We all grab the edge and pry the circular cover from the street. A few people walk past, but no one seems to care about a couple of kids messing with city property. Just New Yorkers, minding their own business.

Below is a dark hole that looks bottomless.

"Okay, Tall," says V, "time to use that tallness for something useful."

"So I'm just here for my height?" he replies.

"You're here because my cousin trusts you. You're

useful 'cause you're tall. The only one tall enough to reach the bottom from the end of the ladder. Now go be useful."

Tall shrugs. "I do prefer that to being useless," he says to me, and plunges down the hole to the sewer below.

Once Tall hollers that he's made it to the ground, V and I climb down the ladder with Tall's help at the bottom.

We snake through the tunnel, staying on the platforms and hanging on to wet bricks to avoid the sludge streaming beneath us. We spot a familiar wooden hatch on the ceiling, spray-painted with a giant red *M*.

"*M* marks the spot," V says. V looks to Too Tall, who is wiping down his shoes with a rag.

"Wish y'all had told me we goin' on a post-game mission, might involve raw sewage, might wanna wear some beaters."

"Mind doing the honors, Your Usefulness?" prods Veronica.

Tall nods, reaches up, and grabs the rusted handle of the wooden hatch.

A blast of cold air hits us as we all look into the opening.

I pull myself up the rungs of another ladder. We climb a set of stairwells into the guts of the Mercury Theater. It gets colder the higher we climb. At the last set of stairs, we see the crystals that have taken over the theater. They drip from the ceiling above us like black icicles.

We turn another corner and the auditorium opens up to us. It's now a cathedral of giant crystals. Inky quartz shards poke through from the floor and ceiling like giant glass daggers. They crisscross in every direction. The shiny surfaces of the matrix of crystals reflect the night sky above. The hole in the domed ceiling shows the faint twinkling of faraway stars.

The husk of the broken Mirror sits center stage. It's like some forgotten science experiment left in the corner of a room for weeks, except instead of mold, it's grown crystals in every direction.

The memories of this place flood me. Pops disappearing, Urma floating through the hole in the roof like a dark butterfly and me diving into that Mirror, into the Realm, and then returning to send Urma back where she came from. Last time I stepped foot in here, we all barely escaped.

This time, we have no plans to leave.

TALL, V, AND I are frozen in place, none of us daring to be the first to walk onto the stage.

V slaps me on the back. "How 'bout you go first, King?"

"Yeah, we'll, uh, keep a lookout down here," Tall adds, his voice cracking.

It's hard to walk through all this crystal. I have to step carefully to avoid the jutting edges, like walking barefoot on gravel. On center stage, there's a cleared circle that's flat like a mown lawn. The Mirror husk is in the center, and crystal blocks stick up in the air within the circle, almost like someone arranged them that way.

"This is super strange, guys," I call down to them.

"Are the tricks there?" calls V.

"Right, the tricks!"

"What's so strange, then?" Tall asks with a loud gulp.

"Better come see for yourselves." I step on the flat circular area toward the Mirror. My foot slips, like I'm walking on ice. I spot three plastic orange labels that say *1, 2, 3*. Must be from the Omega team. I stare into the crystal beneath each label. I can just make out the tricks below in the glow of moonlight. The Deck, the Pistol, and the Skull.

"The tricks are here!" I announce, relieved.

Tall and V approach the flat circle through the stalks of crystals, like stepping through high grass. They edge sideways, holding on to each other like they're creeping through a haunted house.

"Whoa," says V when she sees the circle.

"*Aliens,*" whispers Tall.

We turn to him.

"Sorry, but this has got a creepy crop-circle vibe."

"But how'd it get like that?" I say. "Think it has something to do with these elemental tricks stuck in there?" I tap the crystal above the tricks with my shoe.

"Or is it that?" says V, and points up to the hole in the roof.

Encrusted in crystal, the hole lets in a moonbeam that hits the stage like a spotlight. Maybe the crystal enhances the brightness. On center stage, the moonlight covers about the same space as the flat circle of crystal. "Okay, I see it. Weird."

"So the moon changes the shape of the crystals?" Tall wonders out loud.

"Then these shapes sticking up within the circle? What's up with those?" asks V.

There are five standing blocks within the circle. Three are in a line, and two are just above them.

"Those three in the line look like—nah, it's stupid," says Tall.

"Didn't stop you from saying *aliens* or *crop circles*," V points out.

"Yeah, Tall—spill it."

"I don't know, maybe I just got Orion on the brain 'cause of your uncle. But those three there—they're in a line, but the line is a little off? Reminds me of Orion's Belt."

"Hmm," says V. *"As above, so below."*

"That's what your dad keeps telling me."

"Do you remember how he told you to hold your hands triangle?" I ask Tall.

He blinks twice. *"Hands triangle?"*

"I didn't come up with that, *you* did," I explain. But he doesn't believe me.

"He doesn't remember any of that, King—remember?" V says, and turns to Tall. "My dad told you to find Orion's Belt in the sky and make a triangle with your hands." She makes the delta shape with the tips of her thumbs and index fingers touching.

The lights outside flicker and go out as a blackout rolls over Echo City. The light of the moon slants across V's and Tall's faces.

"Blackout—Long Fingers said we need a blackout!" I say.

I look up through the opening in the roof. The night sky is young, but it looks clear now, and peppered with stars. I take the Echo Stone and hold it up to face the cosmos.

"What're you doing?" asks Tall.

"Trying something—anything. Help me find Orion's Belt!"

Too Tall and Veronica stand next to me, staring up.

"We're running out of time. The blackout's almost over," I say.

"I think we have company," says V.

I hear footsteps and voices coming from the lobby entrance. But I refuse to look away.

"Can you find the North Star?" asks V. "Then you just follow the Big Dipper, right?"

"I think I have it," I say, holding the stone above my head and staring at the three stars of Orion's Belt. *What now? Is something supposed to happen? What am I doing wrong?*

"Excuse me, what are you kids doing in here?"

There's the Omega team. This cornball dude in slacks, loafers, and an orange fed vest with a rack of people who wear boots and carry keys and gear that jingle and clank like futuristic security guards.

Then I remember something Long Fingers said up on the roof . . .

The cosmos doesn't just flip on its axis. It takes thousands of years for the stars to move that much.

"Wait, the North Star—maybe it's not the North Star?" I say.

"What do you mean?" asks V.

"Is this some kinda riddle?" asks Tall.

"Remember, Maestro swapped our cosmos for one from the past. Long Fingers said it takes thousands of years for stars to move like that. Maybe we have a different North Star?"

"Hey, sonny?" says the Omega dude in slacks and loafers. "I asked you a question. You can't be here. I'm going to have to ask you all to leave immediately."

"One way to find out," Tall says. He takes the Echo Stone in his hands and turns it so the point now faces a bright star to the east.

A shaft of blue light beams through the hole in the roof.

It stops Omega team in its tracks.

As the Echo Stone syncs into perfect alignment, a beam of light emanates from the tip and shoots onto the black crystal formation rising from the stage, right smack in the husk of the Mirror. A rectangle of pure light takes shape in the empty space where the Mirror used to be.

"*Whoa*," say V and Tall together.

The energy sends streaks of blue light through the black crystals, making them more translucent and revealing the Skull, the Pistol, and the Deck lit bright beneath the surface.

The rectangle ahead of us opens like an infinite doorway.

About five white-suited security guards with the loafers dude are coming up the stairs and onto the stage. I can see the lights starting to flick on around us and outside. This is our only shot.

"There's only one way to go," I yell back at Veronica and Too Tall.

"You ready?" says V.

"Ready as it gets."

Tall pulls his hat on tight.

I place the Echo Stone around my neck.

"Hold my hands. Keep close to me."

They each take one of my hands. I brace myself in front of the Mirror husk, now glowing with a new portal.

We all jump in.

⚡

LAST TIME I did this, it felt like stepping into a mirror. This time it feels like we're shot out of a cannon. All I can see is light blazing past me, like on the subway tracks, minus the subway. This time, *I'm* the subway. *We're* the subway. I hold on tight to V's and Too Tall's hands, running left, right, up, and down through wormholes like when the express train blows by the station without even pausing. The streaks of light blast by so fast, my eyes can't take it. I hold even tighter. And everything goes black.

I come to, and we're no longer moving. I can feel sunshine, and it's hot. It's hard to open my eyes—everything went from black to blinding white. Then I realize that V's and Too Tall's hands aren't there. I feel something else in my hands. I'm sinking.

Sand.

"I don't think we're in Brooklyn anymore," says Tall.

I look over and can just make out a silhouette of his long legs extending way above me. I get a huge sense of relief. Tall reaches his hand to lift me up.

Next to him, V gives me a hug.

"You okay, cuzzo?"

"I think so," I say, and blink away the dark, trying to adjust to the light, like knives in my eyes.

"Someone's here I think you should see," says V.

"King." Pop's voice is like syrup. "You made it."

MY POPS. NOT an echo of my pops. But the real thing. I know it's him, 'cause you can't grow a beard like that in twenty-six hours. Not with all the salt and pepper and twisties at the ends.

I hug him so fast I barely see the rest of him. I breathe him in. He pulls back to look at me better, and his eyes are watery and I guess mine are, too.

"It's really you," he says.

"It's the real you," I say, our voices overlapping.

The skin around his eyes crinkles.

He takes my hand in his, palm to palm, and touches my knuckles to his heart.

"Last time I saw you, I was almost home," he says.

"I tried to pull you through," I say, remembering when I had his hand back at the Mercury, halfway through the Mirror. "Then Urma happened. And you were gone."

"That was a wild trip," he says, shaking his head at the memory. "Sent me bopping around the echoes like a pinball machine."

"But you landed okay?"

"I guess you could say that," he replies, and then fades away, deeper into another memory, where he sees something foul before coming back. "Only I found an even bigger problem." The Echo Stone around my neck catches his attention. A look of astonishment breaks across his face. "The—the Echo Stone?" Then he realizes something and corrects himself. "Of course. How else could you be here, at the beginning, the alpha?" Pop runs a forefinger and thumb across his brow. "Of course he got an Echo Stone," he says to himself. "The boy walked into the world's first echo. But how?" He looks right at me. "Why are you here? How did you get this?" The questions come on top of one another.

"I—" I stutter, thrown off by his surprise and glancing down at the stone. "I thought you sent it to me."

That makes him pause.

"I'm bringing it back to you," I go on.

He takes the stone in his hands. He stares, as if trying to remember something.

"Could it be?" His voice softens, like he's trying to remember something he's forgotten.

Tall and V stare at Dad like he's a couple deuces short of a full deck.

"Didn't you send it to me?" I ask. Were we wrong? Was all this echo jumping for nothing?

"Maybe," he says, a smile brightening his face.

"Maybe?" I question, glad to see that smile.

"Tell me why you think I sent it to you."

"Well, it's kind of a long story. I met this girl. She's Maestro's daughter, actually."

"You mean Sula?" he says.

For some reason, it feels strange to hear him say her name. Like they're supposed to belong to different worlds. But the worlds turn out to not be different at all.

"And Sol," Veronica chimes in helpfully.

"Wow. Maestro's kids," says Pops, shaking his head.

"Yeah. It's been kinda cool, getting to know them. Sol is sort of magic and sort of messed up, since the Realm Urma was his mom," I say.

"Really," says Pops in a cryptic way.

"He's got this ability to see into the Realm. And then

he paints what he sees. He did this painting on their bath-room wall of you placing the Echo Stone in a box. Then Sula checked this box that her dad had, and it looked the same as your Lost and Found but with a bunch of Egyptian symbols on it."

"Amazing," Dad says.

"So she gave me the stone, 'cause she knew it was from you."

"So Sol *saw me* put this in a box?" says Pop.

"Yeah," says V. "Sol's murals always show what's hap-pening in the Realm."

"Then I must have done it," Pop says, shrugging.

"Mr. James, I hate to be the one to call this out, but shouldn't you be the one who knows that?" asks Too Tall with a wince. "I mean, if you're the one who did it."

"That's a good question." Dad drops a hangdog look at his own hands. "I think this means . . . Either *I'm* an echo of the real Preston. Or I'm trapped in a loop."

The thought jolts me. *Not the real him? Could it be?* But I remember the beard. This *has* to be the real him.

"King and I said the same thing, when we realized," says V.

"Realized what?" asks Pops.

"That we were living in a loop," V explains. "The same

twenty-six hours, over and over. Only every time it resets, we'd forget we'd done it all already."

"I started having crazy déjà vu," I say.

"Wait: That means—*oh, no!*" Dad yells, spins around, and kicks at a top layer of sand. He drops into a squat, hands on his knees. "He did it," Pops declares. "Marcus, he did it."

"What are you saying, Pop?"

But he doesn't respond right away. His eyes are shut tight in concentration.

For the first time since we arrived on solid land—or solid sand, I should say—I have a look around.

There's not much to see. Desert that just goes on and on, on all sides, big as the galaxy. It's so warm, we've all shed our winter coats. There's a formation of tall black stones in the sand behind my dad. The sunset falls from yellow to pink to red, and the shadows from the stones reach like ghouls from the land of the dead.

"Pop—*where are we?*" I ask.

And I realize the pattern in the sand looks similar to something we just saw . . .

A big circle of stones surround five stones set in the center. The five stones are spaced apart in an exact way, forming the same setup as the crystal blocks on the Mercury Theater's center stage.

"I've seen this before," says Too Tall, realizing along with me.

"The Mercury," says V. "The stage floor."

"The circle in the moonlight," I say.

"We're in the Egyptian desert, a place called Nabta Playa," says Pops, opening his eyes and rising to his feet. "These monoliths represent the current position of the cosmos at the moment of the comet strike and the creation of the very first echo." He points to the circle's center.

"Why does it look just like the crystals on the Mercury stage floor?" I ask.

"Does it, now?" Dad says, stroking his beard.

"A dead ringer," says Tall.

"And the crystals at the Mercury—they were all arranged by Urma. She must have made it that way."

"Wait—Urma did that *on purpose*?"

"I believe so," says Dad. "She was helping Maestro. That's the only way it makes sense. For him to cast his spell on our reality, he needs a place that looks like this. Only I didn't know until this moment that what I'm trying to stop from happening tonight has already happened. I haven't even fought Maestro yet, and I've already lost."

"How's that possible?" I ask.

"I—I guess I've been living a loop, starting at the top and forgetting, each time. See, I'm here right now, waiting for Maestro. I'm here to stop him. But if your time is looped, that means I've failed. He stopped time."

"But how?" V pipes up. "How does that work? How does one *stop time*?"

"A ritual," says Dad. "Performed right here, at the stone circle, with the Echo Stone."

"It's a done deal?" asks Tall.

Dad nods, his face like a tombstone. The heat seems to rise off the sand, and I sweat a little behind the ears.

"Maestro is on his way here?" asks V.

Dad nods some more. "That day, when I almost came back with you? There was some kind of explosion of Realm energy. I tried to find my way home. Instead, I found Maestro. I followed him. He was jumping from echo to echo, almost like he was searching for one. I thought he might be trying to reset the timeline, so I tried to take the Echo Stone from him. Only he escaped with the stone into a portal. I held on to him as he jumped. We both ended up here, at the alpha. He's somewhere close by, even now. And now you're here, with that . . ." His thoughts trail off. "Tell me, King, how many times have you lived through a loop?"

I have to think about that. "I'm not exactly sure. At least three times, once I started noticing everything was so familiar. But I couldn't say how many times before that."

Pop looks out over the circle of standing stones. "Then I've had this showdown with Maestro at least as many times."

They fought, I think, *over and over. Every loop, each time I rode the train, ate pizza, and crushed the soda can from the stoop, Pop was here, fighting for his life.* I imagine Pop and Maestro in their eternal war, the way it always seemed when I'd look at the posters of the night of their magic battle.

"The only way this makes sense—that you have an

Echo Stone, and I sent it to you—is if I took the stone from Maestro in one of those battles. I must have dropped it in my Lost and Found box to get it away from Maestro. If Maestro was right on top of me, I wouldn't have had time to make a portal and escape myself."

"Well, great!" says Tall. "If you got the stone from him, shouldn't that make things right?"

"The Realm doesn't work that way," says Pops. "Maestro completed the ritual here, in one of those loops. Even if I stop that from happening in the next loop, it still happened, a done deal, so to speak, until it's undone."

"Here!" I say, offering the stone to Pop. "Take it! Undo the deal!"

"Not so fast, King. Remember, Maestro is *close*. I need you three to listen here, to understand Maestro's plan. In case I fail—"

"You *won't* fail, Pop—you sent me the Echo Stone, don't you see? That means you won," I say.

"But Maestro also stopped time. That means I *did* fail. At least once, anyway. If he and I battle over and over, probably he takes some and I take some. I don't know who wins, when all's said and done. So you got to understand what he's up to," he says, and fidgets with the small hand on the Watch of 13. "Even if he succeeds tonight, you can stop him. Maestro needs to reset three different echoes in the space of a single cycle of twenty-six hours. First, he reset the stone circle here at Nabta Playa." Dad kneels and draws a circle in the sand. "You with me?" he asks.

V, Tall, and I nod.

"He has to reset the echo he wants to make the new prime reality, wherever that is," he explains, and he draws a line connecting to a second circle, with a question mark inside. "And then to finish the spell, he must visit the old prime reality, aka our home, before twenty-six hours is up." He draws a line to a third circle with an *EC* inside, for our Echo City. "There, he'll seal its fate."

Pop stands upright like he's finished the lesson, and watchdogs the horizon.

I look down at the three circles in the sand. Three circles for three echoes.

"Okay, I think I got it. First, here. Then, some random echo. And then back home to our real-life echo. So Maestro may have done the first ritual here to stop time from going forward. But he hasn't performed all three within twenty-six hours."

"Right," says Pops. "I stopped him from the next two steps by sending his Echo Stone to you. See, each time the loop repeats, Maestro possesses just a copy of the Echo

Stone. There's only one. No copy has the raw magical power to reset the cosmos."

"An echo Echo Stone, if you will," cracks Tall. "Sorta like Not Not Ray's Pizza?"

"So what's the echo he wants to make the new prime?" V asks, pointing to the question mark. "Must be some point in history, right?"

My dad frowns and shakes his head. "I've narrowed it down, only I can't be sure. I've thought about it and thought about it. I feel like I *should* know, but we were friends so long ago, and my memory fades."

"Wait, Pops," I say, realizing something terrifying. "If the only thing stopping Maestro from resetting the next echoes is this stone, is it bad that I just brought it back here?"

"You can't think like that, King," he says, kneeling next to me. "This Echo Stone is also the only way to reset the cosmos here at the alpha and set things straight. You did the right thing."

"So can you just do the ritual now and fix it?" I ask, hopeful.

"Not with Maestro on the loose. The ritual takes too much time, requires too much of my attention."

So I did the right thing only if you win, I think, but I say nothing and try to smile.

"May I hold it?" he asks.

I remove the chain over my head, and Dad examines the stone and watch by the light of the setting sun.

"The big hand of the watch will keep track of time in the prime, no matter what echo you jump to," Dad explains.

He points to the big hand, ticking away the minutes in Echo City. In another world, we're home right about now, with Mom joining us and crashing on the couch. He removes the Watch of 13, looks at the back, and then clicks it in place. He finds the latch in the chain and disconnects it. He frees the triangle piece, and hands it to me. "Hold that," he says, and I almost feel like a magician's helper onstage.

Then something stops him cold.

"King," he says in amazement. "Your hand, it's . . . *glowing*?"

I get an ache in my stomach, realizing that as close as I feel to him, we still haven't had time to reconnect. He barely knows me now.

I hold up my glove and slowly take it off, one finger at a time. I watch his amazed reaction, like he's the audience and *I'm* the magician. The pride is overwhelming.

"How'd this happen?" he asks.

"When I first reached into the Magician's Lost and Found, I sorta accidentally blipped open a portal, and I dunno, my hand's been stuck between dimensions ever since. It's magic, I guess. Real magic. Like, I can move things from across the room when I concentrate. It's invisible in the real world, and I guess it just kinda glows here in the Realm."

He holds his hands out together, and without him saying so, I lower my glowing hand to his. He touches my flesh, though he can't see it, and each time, he laughs in amazement, and that makes me laugh, too.

"King, this is extraordinary."

"You think?"

"Without a doubt," he declares, and beams.

Dad checks the sky once more. The sun is almost down, with one last stab of light piercing the horizon.

"When this is over, you'll tell me all about everything, okay, King? I mean *everything*," he says, and winks.

I nod as he draws the chain to its full length and stares at each link. He slowly spools the chain into his open palm. He closes both hands together so the chain is collapsed inside his cupped hands. He shakes his hands and closes his eyes to focus.

He opens his hands and reveals the chain, but it's transformed. It's still a chain, but the links are twice as big, and there are two heavy metal cuffs on each end.

"*Whoa,*" says Tall.

"Shackles?" says Veronica.

"That's like OG magic-dude magic," Tall whispers to me in awe.

"Are those for who I think they're for?" I ask.

"The Echo Stone and its chain are made from the only material that can hold him," says Dad. He takes the stone and puts it inside his jacket pocket, close to his chest. "I'll keep this right here. Now, hide, everyone. He's coming."

IF THE STONE circle were a clock, Too Tall, V, and I are hiding behind stones seven, eight, and nine o'clock. Tall had to take the tallest monolith to hide him. My pops is behind a stone over by three o'clock. A figure approaches at the imaginary twelve o'clock.

The first thing I see is the headdress, with horns on either end. It's Maestro, but the headdress makes him look seven feet tall. The sun is all the way down, but I can see him by the blue highlight of the stars. It's like they're surging extra bright. I see now that Maestro's headdress is the shape of a single arm with hands on the tips like the ref calling a field goal. It's that thing I saw Sol painting back in Echo City. The symbol of Heka, the god of magic. Or was it magic itself?

He's naked from the waist up with a traditional-looking sash around his hips. There are markings all over his body. That's not at all how I remember him. He used to have these small, fidgety eyes that would dart around like somebody stole something. Now he has this serene face with eyes clear and calm as the horizon. He even moves different. He used to perform onstage with these awkward jerks and gestures. Now he walks like he's barely trying. His arms are straight at his sides, and his knees are held close together in the sash, but he's gliding smooth and fast across the desert floor, making waves in the sand like a pair of snakes are following him.

The air shifts as he approaches the circle. The standing stones tremble in the sand floor.

Then Dad steps into the center, holding out his flat hand.

"Stop," he says. "I can't let you do this."

I swallow a breath of panic. *What is he doing? Does he really think that's going to work with Maestro?*

"Preston," says Maestro in a calm voice to match his unshakable look. "You don't understand what I intend to do."

"I've known you a long time, Marcus."

"No one knows me," says Maestro with a shrug. "I am unknowable."

"What you plan to do here—it's not right."

"Not right? Right, wrong—such relative words. And such a waste of time."

He steps so he's shoulder to shoulder with the stones of the circle.

"What I am going to do cannot be prevented," he says.

"Not when I have this," says my dad, and he holds up the Echo Stone.

Maestro stops cold. His expression doesn't change. He's at the lip of the circle, but he hasn't crossed that boundary. Not yet. He seems to pause to think about it.

Then he smiles.

As soon as Maestro's foot crosses into the stone circle, my father vanishes.

He appears instantly behind Maestro.

Faster than I can blink, he takes Maestro by the wrist and slaps the handcuffs on him.

Maestro tumbles away from my father, arms trapped behind his back, like he got arrested at an Egyptian cosplay party.

I let out a huge breath that I only just realize I was even holding in.

Maestro—he'd seemed so dangerous, so powerful before. And I was terrified by the way Dad was talking to him—like he could just talk him out of whatever wild mission he was on. Even I knew that wouldn't work on Maestro. I was hoping Dad knew something I didn't. Turns out he did.

I try to piece together how Dad even did the misdirection. Was he ever in the center of the circle? Or was that some kind of illusion the whole time? Perhaps as he cast the illusion of himself, he snuck up around the stones . . .

I'm tempted to come out into the circle and celebrate, but I want to wait for Pops to give the say-so. I hope Tall and Veronica do the same.

Maestro has sunk down to one knee, wrists locked behind his back.

"The chain, the chain of the Echo Stone," says Maestro. "I was wondering where it was when you showed me the stone. Clever, Preston. Worthy of you." He laughs at the bitterness of losing to his rival once more.

"I'm sorry, Marcus. I couldn't let you."

"Let me what? Make a world where magic is the one true religion?"

"We would lose too much," my dad says sadly.

"You don't know that!" Maestro raises his voice for the first time. His tone has been calm until now.

"It's not something I can risk," says Dad.

"You're a fool, Preston!" Maestro shouts. "You'll still be a fool after the Great Shift!"

He laughs with a manic look in his eyes and removes his hands from behind his back.

He's holding a serpent made of stone . . .

But it's moving. Slithering. Waving its head back and forth like it's taunting Dad.

I don't know how that's possible.

I catch myself wondering, *Where's the chain?* before realizing: *The serpent is the chain. He changed it again.*

"H-how?" Dad sounds horrified.

"I have my own," says Maestro.

He reaches to his waist and fingers the knot of his sash. He detaches something that was hanging from the belt and holds up a chain with another Echo Stone with the Watch of 13 lodged inside.

"How?" Dad repeats. He looks at the Echo Stone in his jacket pocket.

There's no watch on it . . .

It's the copy, I realize with horror. *When Dad cuffed him, Maestro switched them, sleight of hand . . .*

He has the true Echo Stone!

"Did you really think I wouldn't detect this?" Maestro sneers. "That which revealed itself to me?"

Maestro flings the snake at my dad.

The snake snares Pop by the wrist and wraps around his arm like a bracelet.

Maestro raises his fingers with a twist, and the snake—or chain, I guess—stretches Pop's arm up over his head, like he's got the answer in class.

Maestro jerks the chain off his stone, and it snaps into another snake, rock-solid and hissing. He catches the now-disconnected Echo Stone with his other hand as it falls.

He flings the second serpent at Dad, and that one slaps around his other wrist. Then the two serpents conjoin and attach behind Dad's back. They pull him backpedaling into a stone monolith and hold him there.

Maestro whispers words that hiss. *"The sky trembles. The earth quakes before him. The Magician is Maestro. Maestro possesses magic."*

A chill hits the air.

Dad, I think. *I have to help.*

But how?

You've got no time! No time! Help him now!

And then another voice insists, *Don't be a fool! Hide!*

With the thoughts raging blind in my mind, I step into the circle and reach my gloved hand toward the snakes. I think, *Release him,* with all the power I ever thought I had and then some. I'm straining; I can feel the muscles in my neck tense and quiver.

Maestro smirks. "Release him, young one?" he says, and reaches a hand back out at me, the way I'm doing, almost like he's imitating me.

A force lifts me off my feet and sends me slamming into the stone behind me. I try to move, but I can't. It's like I'm held in place by some irresistible magnetic power. I feel the rough grooves of stone dig into my back.

"King, no!" shouts Too Tall.

He steps into the circle, ready to charge, but as soon as he does, Maestro twists his fingers like he's flicking a pinch of salt, and Tall slams against the nearest circle stone.

"Ah, I can't move!" he says.

Maestro turns to the Echo Stone in his open palm. He removes the Watch of 13. "Adorable," he says, and tosses it in the sand.

"I have come," Maestro begins in a chant, *"that I may take possession of my throne and that I may receive my dignity, for to me belonged all before you came into being."*

Glowing with refracting light, the stone levitates away from his hand and drifts toward the center of the circle, where it spins.

"You gods, go down and come upon the blacker parts, for I am a magician."

Everything around us changes.

The night isn't the night anymore.

The sky isn't the sky.

It's the entire cosmos. And it's wide awake. It's blinking and breathing all around us, slipping like skin moving along the scalp.

The only thing that's the same is what's inside the standing stone circle. Dad, trapped in chains, and Maestro in his goalpost headdress, levitating now and chanting to the spinning stone.

"For to me belonged the universe before you came into being. I am 'if-he-wishes-he-does.' Descend, you who have come in the end. I am Heka."

THE ECHO STONE spins and spins. Then it stops, and it feels like the world around us spins instead. Then it's like the entire stone circle is what's spinning, and the entire universe around us is still, but it's an Earth-revolves-around-the-sun sort of situation. Just like with the sun, I see the world itself rise and fall around us, when really it's probably just us moving.

The very tip of the Echo Stone shoots a bright light up into the heavens.

There's an explosion of starlight. Everything goes white, like the whole galaxy got dunked in milk.

Then it's over. The lights are gone. The spinning, all that movement, stops. The stars dim to their normal glow.

It feels like when you're underwater and you come up for air and take that first breath.

Maestro hovers back down to the ground. He's heaving.

"It's done," he says to my father.

Pops just shakes his head, shackled and trembling to the bone.

Maestro holds up a hand, and my dad's bag flies to him. He opens the bag and takes out my dad's Magician's Lost and Found.

"And thanks for this, Preston. This makes my next step much easier."

He then pulls at the sides of the box itself, and the wood shatters and splits apart in his hands.

A portal appears where the box once was. A perfect rectangle of glowing blue Realm energy, about the size of his old Mirror.

How did he . . . ?

And I realize he must have ripped open the mini portal of the Magician's Lost and Found.

So much power . . .

Maestro takes his Echo Stone, cups it in his hands, and stares at it with a smile like he's done this before. A whirl of images fills the stone—but he's too far away, and I can't make out anything but dancing lights.

He ducks his Heka headdress, steps through the portal, and is gone.

I immediately fall from the pillar.

Maestro's magic held me there, and Maestro isn't here anymore.

Tall also lands in the sand, on his knees.

"What in the world was *that*?" he asks me.

"I dunno, Tall," I say, getting to my feet.

Veronica appears from behind her stone. "You guys okay?" she asks.

"Where were you?" asks Tall.

"Hiding," she says, without saying the *duh* part out loud.

When she sees we're fine, she rushes to my dad. We're right behind her.

"Uncle P, are you okay?" she asks.

My dad is still shaking his head. I realize there are tears in his eyes.

I hurry to his shackles and try to pull at them. Too Tall helps me. But it's no use.

"The portal!" my dad shouts. "He's closing it!"

I turn to see the rectangular blue portal shrinking in front of us.

"What? H-how?" I stutter.

"With magic!" Dad snaps. "Stop it!"

"Stop it? How?" I ask.

"Magic! Your hand, King, your hand!"

I run to the portal as fast as I can. I have no clue what to do.

Your hand, King, your hand repeats in my mind.

So I reach with my hand. I feel the pull of the portal like a vacuum cleaner trying to suck me in.

I try to stop it from closing the way you stop the subway doors from closing. I just shove my hand in there and hope for the best.

My gloved hand vanishes in the pool of blue energy so all I can see is the end of my wrist at the edge of this blue rectangle.

But the portal has stopped shrinking. It doesn't pop back open like the subway doors, but it's holding steady around my wrist.

This feels so strange.

I try to flex my fingers, but instead of feeling them individually, the blue rectangle flares a few shades brighter. It looks like it should burn hot, but I only feel a cool, steady tingle.

"Well done, King!" I hear my dad behind me. "You have to go through now. All of you."

"Not without you, Pops," I say.

I turn to look at him. He's slumped at the foot of the stone, shoulders hunched over his crossed legs.

Tall and Veronica try to help him out of the cuffs.

"They're, like, stuck!" says Veronica.

"They won't even wiggle!" says Tall.

"You won't be able to break those," says Pops.

"What about your magic?" I ask. "I mean, you were able to, like, morph the other chain."

"No good. Those links are made from the chain of Maestro's Echo Stone. One he apparently discovered himself," Dad says. "The copy is powerless against the original."

He makes a quick movement with his torso and his chest. Almost like he's dancing in a Hula-Hoop. Something drops from inside his jacket and lands on the sand by his feet.

It's the copy of the stone.

"Veronica," my dad says. "Grab the Watch of 13 and reconnect it to this stone. It's a copy, but its magic should still work to navigate the Realm."

V plucks the Watch of 13 up from the sand and connects it to the Echo Stone. Then she looks at Dad like, *You sure about this?*

"It can't reset the cosmos or anything," he says, "but as long as you're all touching each other and the stone, you'll travel through the echoes together, like you did when you came here. Only, after a cycle of twenty-six hours, it will be useless. So do exactly as I say: Move the small hand to the 13 . . . Now move it back exactly seven clicks."

Veronica does as she's told with a trembling finger.

"That's it. If that's the echo I think it is, you'll understand more when you get there. Now hurry. King can't hold that portal open much longer. It will suck him through or close."

"Not without you, Pop!" I shout, louder this time.

"He got the best of me," Dad says, shaking his head. "But not you. You're the ace up my sleeve, King."

"But what do we do?" I ask.

"You know what to do. Find him. He's gone to some echo to make the new prime reality. He must perform this ritual again there, at that echo. It's not over yet, King. You can stop him."

"*Me*? But, Pops, he beat *you*. I brought his Echo Stone right back to him! How do I even stand a chance?"

"Don't worry about that. You took a risk. If I'd won, I could have reversed the ritual with the stone, all because you were brave enough to bring it to me. It's not your fault I lost. Now listen to me: Your hand. Your invisible hand, King. Invisible things are more important, stronger than the visible. The form of a person, what we wear and how we appear—that's only a reflection of what we can't see."

"You're saying I'm stronger because my hand is invisible?" I ask, doubtful.

"All the most important things are invisible, King. Can you see thoughts? Feelings? Can you see justice? Can you see love?"

I shake my head.

"Your magic is in the invisible, Kingston. That's why you can beat Maestro. It's the power of what we cannot see."

I realize how much I've missed him, and that I'm about to say goodbye again.

"Uncle P, I don't feel good about just leaving you like this," says Veronica.

"I know, V. None of this feels right because everything has gone wrong. You shouldn't have to clean up the mess that your dad and I couldn't fix ourselves."

"That feels okay, Unc. The problems you and my dad couldn't fix are the most important." She shrugs and looks over the stone and watch, then comes and takes me by the hand.

"You too, Eddie," says my dad.

Too Tall is still yanking at my dad's cuffs, trying to help

free him. "Mr. P, I feel like I could get it—" he says, straining with all his might.

"You can't," says Dad. "Not in a million years. But you can help my son. Please."

Tall nods and surrenders. He comes and takes Veronica's free hand, interlocking his fingers with hers.

"We can't just leave you here, Pop!" I cry out.

"Don't worry about me at all," he says with a twinkle. "You forget what this place is? At the twenty-sixth hour, I'll do it all again. Except this next time, you're here. So don't feel bad for me, King. I'll get to spend all this time with you."

"But—"

"Stop Maestro from completing the ritual before twenty-six hours runs out. Or that will be the last of our reality."

"But how do I find him? He has the Echo Stone, so he could be in any echo."

"You must learn about him. It's the only way to defeat him. To understand what makes him do what he does. He's like the watch, King. He has a mechanism that keeps him ticking, an idea that pushes him forward. He wants a world where magic reigns supreme, and he'll do anything to make that happen. That's his strength, and his weakness. Understand that, and you will win, my son. Go now, King! Go!"

I nod, and as if the portal obeys my littlest thought, it sucks us back into the moving corridors of the Realm.

THE PORTAL SPITS us tumbling into moonlit grass. I get a shot of dirt up my nose. I roll and bump into Tall.

"Where are we?" he asks.

"*Shh,*" says V, her shush blending with faraway and not-so-faraway crickets. She's on her feet, hunched over us. "We don't know who's around."

"Who's around?" says Tall, smacking a bug on his head. "Ow!"

We're in the front yard of a house, late at night. By the light of the den window we see bugs everywhere. Midges, gnats, mosquitoes, you name it.

"Oh man," says V, "I hate bugs."

"Nobody likes bugs," I say. "That's why they're called *bugs*, not *hugs*."

The den window's curtains are open, revealing a familiar living room.

"Wait a minute," I say.

I look up at the house. There's a long porch out front with tall, gothic columns in chipped white paint.

"I know where we are," I say.

A face appears in the window.

"Hold still," I whisper, and I freeze in place.

The light cast from the window ends in the grass just before my feet, and I hope we're hidden in the darkness.

I don't want my mom to see me.

She's there in the window looking out. Younger than I ever knew her.

I glance at Tall and V. They see her, too. They slide their eyes back at me, not daring to move.

I know this place. We used to come to Georgia to stay out here and visit Grandpa Freddy. I'd play outside, and that's how I learned what real grass and trees and nature were all about. And there were gnats. I sort of remember the gnats, but not like how they're torturing me now.

Young Ma opens the window a crack.

Did she hear us?

"Preston?" she calls out. "Is that you?"

Young Ma gives the grass outside a curious look before she shuts the window and walks away.

"King, you know where we are?" asks Tall.

"Georgia," V says. "We used to visit when we were kids."

I check the Echo Stone in my hand. The Watch of 13's small hand is pointing up between the 12 and the 13. A bug flies into my eye. I take a swing and swat myself in the face.

Before Tall can even laugh at me, he smacks himself in the cheek for the same reason.

"I hate this," V says, scratching all over her body, even over her sleeves. "They're crawling on my brain. Can we get inside or something?"

"Why don't we just ring the bell, say hi?" Tall suggests. "I'm sure they'll be nice to us. Maybe give us something to eat? You could hang with your mom?"

"No, Tall," I say. "We can't mess with them."

"Why not? I mean, they're just echoes, right? They forget everything twenty-six hours later, right?"

"Because if we talk to them, they may not do what they're supposed to. What the echo copied. Then we might mess up whatever we're here to see, follow me?"

"Uh . . ."

"My dad had V put this location in the Echo Stone for us. He wanted us to come here. We have to find out why."

"Okay, but if the bugs devour us alive, we can't find out anything," says V.

"Let's try the back door," I say, remembering the back porch entrance.

We sneak around and walk through a door onto the old screened-in porch. There's a dusty stack of newspapers on the coffee table. I glance at the date—July 24, 2003.

Before V and I were even born.

I hear footsteps coming from inside the house itself, and we hide behind some wicker furniture. It's Dad, in an old pair of leather house slippers, an ancestor of the worn-out slippers I remember in Brooklyn. I can only see him from the ankles down. I wonder, what does he looks like? Did he have his goatee then? I wonder, when he was that age, did he ever do something as stupid as, say, bring his worst enemy the one thing he needs to win, like I did with Maestro's Echo Stone?

Pops sits on one of the porch chairs with a crunch, and I hold my breath.

I hear Mom from inside the house.

"Oh, you're out here?"

"Yeah, babe. Just had an idea for something for my act, going to tinker a bit."

"Okay. Well, don't tinker too long."

They exchange "good nights" and "love yous" and they sound just like they did when I was young.

But "I" haven't happened just yet.

Pops kicks off those slippers and stretches his toes. I hear the flick of a lighter as cigar smoke fills the screens surrounding the back porch.

My mom hates those cigars.

So this is what he meant by "tinker a bit."

"Preston," a soft voice echoes from inside. *"Preston,"* says a man's voice, though I barely hear it.

Dad's feet slap the floor and slide into his slippers.

He heads back inside the house in a hurry.

I look over at Tall, folded up into a fetal ball, knees pressed tight to his chest so he tucks beneath the reclining lounge chair. V is crouched behind a lawn chair to my left.

"Who's that?" V whispers.

I shrug. "Dunno."

"My knees are killing me," whispers Tall.

"You prefer the bugs in the yard?" I ask.

"I'd prefer food," he answers.

I roll my eyes.

"I gotta go check this out," I whisper. "You two stay here, and stay outta sight. I'll be right back."

Tall holds up a fist, and then points to his mouth and makes a chewing motion.

Veronica squints at me.

Why do you get to go? she seems to ask.

Because it's my dad, I think, and for some reason, I feel like she hears me.

Hurry, she answers.

But she doesn't actually say a word.

The warmth of the old house hits me as I pad quietly through the kitchen. A fire burns in the fireplace in the other room.

"Preston." I hear the man's voice again, like it's coming from upstairs.

My father thinks the same thing, climbing the staircase.

I pause at the fridge and take a peek. There's a box labeled *MoonPies*, with a picture of what looks like a s'more dipped in chocolate. My stomach gurgles at the sight of it, and I almost grab one, until someone's voice snaps me out of it.

"Babe, did you say my name?" I hear my dad ask from upstairs.

My mom mumbles something in the negative. Pops comes back out as I sneak toward the staircase myself.

"Preston," the voice calls again.

Dad goes up another level, to the attic.

I tiptoe after him.

"Preston," the voice calls.

And Dad's voice answers.

"What in Houdini and Herman are you doing here?" says Pops. He sounds flustered.

I sneak up to the attic staircase and sit right at its foot.

"Preston! You can hear me? It worked!" says the other voice.

Maestro.

He sounds delirious, like he's fresh from some awe-inspiring experience.

But here? In Georgia? I have no memory of Maestro ever being here. What is he even doing in the attic? And why didn't Dad know where he was in the house?

"I can hear you and see you," says Dad.

"Extraordinary!" Maestro celebrates. "Preston, I have to tell you—Black Herman did it!"

"Did what?" says Dad. "And how'd you get *here*? In my granddad's mirror? Marcus, how are you doing this?"

"I'm in the Realm, Preston. I'm stuck. I need you to open a portal and bring me home."

I CLIMB, AS close as I dare, up the attic steps. I peer just above the top step and can see over my dad's shoulder.

It's an old mirror. Instead of reflecting the attic and my father, Maestro's image is in the glass.

"I've learned so much about magic and the Realm," he says, his awkward body language so different from the wild, half-naked wizard I saw at Nabta Playa. "There are places where reflections thin the veil between worlds. Mirrors of a certain proportion can be accessed from either side. Preston, there's so much to tell! I met Black Herman."

"Yeah, okay," says Dad.

"No, not in that way. Not an echo, not a copy. It's him,

in the flesh, Preston. He's alive, and in the Realm! He did it!"

"Did what?"

"He achieved immortality!"

Maestro's voice loops up with excitement like a roller coaster.

"What? What are you saying?" says Dad, but his voice has changed. He sounds eager and curious. Maestro has him on the hook.

"I know it sounds impossible. But the crowds in Louisville, in 1934, were right. Black Herman faked his own death. In the end, that was his greatest trick! Like the old pharaohs, don't you see? The Egyptians—the original magicians, they knew it all along, how to live forever! Please, bring me home, and I can explain."

"Okay," says Dad, taking a step away from Maestro. He glances around the attic, and I duck back down a couple steps. "I need more room."

The mirror scrapes off the attic floor as he picks it up.

I hurry down the steps to stay ahead of him.

As quickly and quietly as possible, I step across the wall-to-wall carpeting to the screened-in back porch.

Only Pops seems like he's following me.

Veronica and Too Tall scurry back to their hiding places as I open the door.

"I totally saw both of you," I whisper as I get to my own hiding spot.

Pops takes the mirror to the backyard and sets it down in the grass up against a tree trunk. Its frame catches heaps of moonlight, since it's made of solid crystal.

Pops turns around and heads back inside.

"What's he doing?" asks Tall once he's out of range.

"He's about to bring Maestro back from the Realm," I say.

Tall and V perk up. If they were rabbits, their ears would be straight to the ceiling.

I explain everything I heard in the attic.

Tall puts it together. "So he's gonna bring Maestro home like how you almost brought your dad home this summer?"

"Something like that, yeah," I say.

"But why are we here?" asks V. "How does this help us stop Maestro now?"

"I dunno, V. I mean, we got to find him first, right? He's in one of these echoes. Maybe Dad's trying to point us in the right direction? He said we have to learn why he does what he does. What makes him tick. That's how we'll win. I bet something happens here that's important," I say. "Otherwise, Dad wouldn't have sent us."

"He's coming," whispers V.

Pops comes back out carrying a familiar old magician's chest. He sets it down in the grass and waves at some bugs and swats himself in the head. Tall shrugs at me, nodding. Pops takes out his famous three tricks: the Skull, the Deck, and the Pistol. He then sets them down on the grass so they make a triangle around the mirror.

The mirror fills with blue light as the tricks levitate off the ground.

The rest of the portal ceremony is all too familiar to me by now.

Same with Pops, it seems. He knows exactly what to do. He reaches into the blue-lit glass, and his hand descends into the pool of light up to his wrist. I half expect him to come out with no hand, like mine. But instead, he comes out holding Maestro's hand. The rectangular mirror doesn't look big enough for a whole body to fit through, but space doesn't mean much when it comes to portal magic. With my dad's arm for support, Maestro steps all the way out of the mirror and falls to his knees on the grass.

"Thank you, Preston," he says, eyes tearing with relief.

Dad helps him up. "You okay, you wild wizard?"

"All in one piece, I think," says Maestro.

Dad looks at the open portal to the Realm hovering in his backyard. "Wow. How am I going to explain *that* to Nina?"

"Give it twenty-six hours, it'll be gone," says Maestro.

"Small comfort," Dad mutters. He sighs, like he's got a problem on his hands. I imagine Mom waking up to an interdimensional portal in their backyard and start to get why Mom isn't magic's biggest fan.

"Well, I could try something," says Maestro. He unbuttons his rumpled shirt and takes it off, revealing his skinny torso.

"Marcus?" asks Dad.

Maestro has a daring look as he approaches the portal. He shakes his open button-down like a matador and drapes the shirt over the old, crystal-framed mirror. Then, in a blink, he pulls the shirt away and snaps it into a ball.

The portal is gone.

My dad looks stunned. "How'd you—" But he doesn't finish his thought; he just grins.

"The portal is still there," says Maestro, putting his shirt back on and glancing at the now normal-looking, crystal-framed mirror. "It's a glamour trick. I learned it by imitating the Realm. Sometimes a portal will appear in just a flash, and vanish. But it's still there, only the

Realm hides it all on its own, like a mirror in a box trick."

"You've learned a thing or two," Dad observes.

"There are ways to manipulate the Realm, ways we've never even considered. The possibilities, Preston. I have so much to tell you," Maestro says with pride, almost like he's gloating. He steps up onto the porch and eyes my dad's setup with his cigars.

I hold my breath, hoping he won't spot us.

"Give me one of those cigars. This is cause for celebration."

Maestro sits on the lounge chair, and the back smooshes into Tall, who holds deathly still.

I can only just see Maestro's outline from behind in the flaring light of his cigar.

"Now tell me," says Dad. "You've been gone over a month. I didn't know if I'd ever see you again. Where have you been?"

"Preston, while you were here, lounging in the sticks," Maestro says, like he's enjoying this, "I rode echo upon echo and saw things I barely believe myself. One jump, and I arrived at Black Herman's Private Graveyard. He's *there*, Preston, for eternity, as far as I can tell. The only problem, he explained to me, is that he can't ever leave. He'll live forever, as long as he stays in that one echo."

"Wow. And what makes that possible?"

"He wouldn't say, not outright. But I understand from him that it has to do with the Missing Key—"

"The Missing Key? As in—"

"The original. The very first. From 1923," says Maestro.

But what are they talking about? What's this *Missing Key*? Why the original?

"So that's going to be your next stop?" my dad asks, not missing a beat, apparently.

"Am I that obvious?" asks Maestro.

"Maybe. Or I just know you, that's all."

"Or you're thinking the same as me," Maestro says. "By my calculations, 1923 is nine echoes away from us now."

"Nine. We could jump nine." My dad gets excited as he lowers his voice, as if he doesn't want Mom to hear.

"Preston! *Immortality*—what's the point of any magic next to that? These tricks, these silly shows night after night, just to fool more fools. We're not magicians to be mere entertainers, are we?" Maestro says.

Pops is quiet, like he doesn't know how to answer that.

"You have something to eat?" Maestro asks like he never expected an actual answer. "I'm famished!"

"Sure, come on inside," Pops says, and opens the porch

door. "The cigar stays out here. Unless you got some new magic that hides cigar smoke, too."

Maestro hops in after my dad, and the screen door winds shut after him.

Too Tall unfolds, stretches his legs out, and lies on his back with a huge sigh of relief. "Tallness," he says, rubbing his knees, "has some definite drawbacks."

"There's our way out," says V, pointing to the crystal-framed mirror outside. "Did you hear what he said? The portal is hidden, but it's still open. If we jump in and work the stone, we won't have to try and make our own portal."

"Okay, I'm with that," says Tall. "Portal making is a pain. Elements, math—it's magic, but it feels like homework."

"But where would we go?" I ask.

"You heard what he said about 1923, nine echoes away?"

"The Missing Key," I say. "Yeah. I caught that. Only, how do we pick that echo, specifically?"

V holds up the Echo Stone. She points to the small hand on the Watch of 13. "Nine echoes away . . . So maybe if we click the small hand nine times, counterclockwise?" she says, ready to do just that.

"V!" I say.

"What?" she asks.

"Nothing. Just, be careful."

"Of all of us, who's the most careful?" she asks point-blank as Too Tall moves to get up off the floor, bangs his head on the lounge chair, and says, *"Oof."*

"Point taken."

"I would like to cast a vote for the plan to go chow before we jump into this next echo," says Too Tall, rubbing his head.

"There is no such plan for you to vote for," says V.

"Then I would like to propose—"

"Tall, my dad and Maestro are in there."

"But why does that matter? They're only echoes, and we know what we need to know, don't we?"

"They have no idea who we are, Big Bird! We aren't even born yet, remember? They'll report us to the cops or something, like this is a home invasion," says V.

"Or they'll cast a spell on us," says Tall, pulling a quick one-eighty and agreeing to V's point.

"Here, Tall. Merry Christmas," I say, and toss a pack of MoonPies to him that I snagged from the fridge earlier. His face opens up like an unwrapped present. "Eat up. Then we got to go. Get ready for another jump."

LANDING IN AN echo is always a new experience. Sometimes the smells hit you first, sometimes the sounds. This time, it's the sole of a bigfoot sneaker smashed into my left cheek.

I flip my hand in front of my eyes, but I can't see a thing. I'm bent up like a pretzel and stuffed into a tight space.

There's a thud and a groan—sounds that go together like lightning and thunder. The sounds of Too Tall smacking his head on something.

"Get off, you're crushing me," says V, apparently wedged beneath me.

"Where am I supposed to go?" says Tall.

"You're only making things worse," V yells at him.

I glimpse a seam of light marking a door or a hatch.

"Where are we?" Tall asks. "What's this chain?"

There's a click, and a light comes on. I blink away the glare from an old-timey bulb.

One of the walls is a mirror, and our faces are staring back.

The rest of the walls are covered in etchings and sketches, like the walls of the public bathroom by Pocket Playground. Numbers and words are cobbled together that make no sense. There are some random geometric shapes and, of course, Egyptian hieroglyphs.

"Great, more nonsense to decode," Tall says.

Every time he makes the slightest movement, Veronica and I get squished into a different corner.

"Can you just be still?" Veronica struggles to turn her head and look around the tiny space. "The mirror, the light bulb . . ." She knocks on one side of the wall. "It's hollow. A false door." She pauses. "I think we're in a spirit cabinet. There should be a release somewhere in here. Look for a handle or a pulley or something."

"I got something," Tall says, pulling on a black rope above his head.

Before we can respond, the bottom drops out beneath

us. We spill onto a hardwood floor like a bag of marbles. V and I squirm away from Tall's giant frame and stretch our legs.

"You can thank me later," Tall says, pushing himself off the ground.

I rub my eyes and take in our new surroundings. We're in a big room with high ceilings. Massive maroon drapes cover the windows on one side. A few lamps scatter pockets of light. Glass jars stuffed with dried herbs cover one table, and plants on another side of the room hang from the rafters. I realize we're in a magician's space. The sweet smell of incense wafts over us. There's tricks and stage props, outfit changes and mounted swords, throwing daggers wedged in a block of wood, cages with fluttering and heavy-breathing creatures, candles melting on the heads of skulls, and a stuffed raven glaring with shiny black marble eyes.

"Uh, think I liked it better where we came from," says Tall.

The spirit cabinet behind us stands a head above Too Tall, made of charcoal-black wood like it was carved from the trunk of a torched tree. There's a pyramid engraved on top with rows and rows of more strange symbols.

"I've seen this before," says V. "My dad was trying to build one. He called it the Cabinet of Souls." She drops her voice and growls just like her father. "The Lamborghini of Magic Cabinets."

"Well, the interior could be a little more comfortable," Tall says.

I go to the window and open the enormous drapes. They must be two stories high. Light spills into the room.

Not daylight, but city lights.

Outside the window is another world. It's like an old black-and-white movie, except everything is in full color. Neon signs flicker with names like Savoy and Cotton Club. The crowds spread from the sidewalk to the street, and lines of people are dressed like this is the most important night of their lives. Pin-striped suits, hats, and color popping off freshly clean dresses. No jeans and no sneakers.

Tall breaks the silence. "What is this place?"

"I'm pretty sure it's New York, but not, like, our New York," I say.

"It's Harlem," says V.

"Hello, 1923," I say.

I look down at the Watch of 13. The big hand tick-ticks away. We're already down to twenty hours.

Then I see a sign on the side of the building, over the line of folks. *Master of Legerdemain,* it reads in a font like one used on an old bottle of medicine. *The Great Black Herman.*

"We're backstage at one of Black Herman's shows," I say. "The Cabinet of Souls? He would roll it out and perform with that thing. This might even be, like, his dressing room. The Missing Key—it must be around here somewhere."

"King," says V, "we don't even know exactly what we're looking for."

"What? A key?" asks Tall, scanning the area.

Footsteps approach from outside the door to the room.

"We got company!" V whispers urgently.

She pulls the drapes around us, and we hide behind them.

The door creaks, and I peek through an opening in the cloth. A shaft of light slants into the room, followed by the roar of a crowd. A boy, probably a stagehand, appears.

He grabs a few things—bottles of herbs and potions— and loads them onto a cart. He's about to head out when he stops and looks back into the room. He stares for what feels like an eternity.

"He saw us," Tall whispers.

"*Shh!*" V kicks him, and I notice his giant feet poking out from under the curtain.

Now the boy is just inches away. He's wearing a news- boy cap and a black button-up shirt that's a few sizes too big. We hold our breaths. I catch him looking back toward the door. I can see his face now. He's just a kid, maybe younger than us.

"What're y'all doing back there?" he whispers. "I can see your feet. Six of 'em. So that makes three of y'all. How'd y'all get in?" He has a laid-back, amused way of speaking, like folks down South.

Veronica shrugs like she's ready to throw in the towel. She steps out.

"Hi, I'm V. Back there is my cousin King and his buddy Too Tall. We're not spies or thieves, just some kids who are lost. We're fans of Mr. Herman, so we tried to sneak in. Then we got caught. And now, here's you."

Tall and I emerge behind V.

"Hi," I say. "I'm King, and that's Too Tall. But you can just call him Tall."

"Hi." Tall waves his hand like an ostrich wing.

The kid takes us in like a long drink of water. He's hardly blinked, and I can't read him.

I'm wondering, *Will he notice that V's story doesn't make sense? Like, are we lost, or did we sneak in?*

"Did y'all come from there?" he says, pointing to the cabinet.

Not what I was expecting. How could he know we came from the cabinet?

"From where?" I ask.

"The cabinet."

"What's that supposed to mean?"

"Well, seen some wild things come through that cabinet, and clearly, y'all are not from around here. Or anywhere I been. What're those clothes? The big guy is wearing pajamas in the evening, and he's got a pair of bathtubs on his feet."

I glance at the white of Too Tall's Taxi 12s. The kid's got us there. I figure maybe we should try another approach— honesty.

I lean closer and lower my voice to a whisper, glancing right to left. "We're looking for the Missing Key."

"Black Herman's *Missing Key*?" he says at full volume. "Why didn't you say so? They got it out front in the lobby."

The three of us breathe with relief. Didn't expect it to be that easy.

"Only . . . ," says the kid.

And here's the catch.

"It's almost intermission, and it'll be gone by then. Better get on your way."

"When's intermission?" asks V.

"Usually after the snake."

"The snake?" Tall steps back. "What snake?"

"Wrong question. *When* is the snake?" corrects V.

"Up next," the kid says.

V marches toward the door.

"Wait. If you just walk out, I'm sure one of the ushers will ask where your parents are. And if you don't got no parents, they'll probably put you with the police, and then who knows where you'll end up tonight. Maybe an orphanage. Or"—he drops a wink—"you can follow me."

We follow the kid out the door, down a short hallway, and through a big door that leads us backstage. We're
behind a massive curtain, and I hear sudden *ooh*s followed
by breathless quiet and then *wow*s as throngs of people are
apparently amazed on the other side.

Is he there? I wonder. *Just there? In the flesh, in his
prime?*

The kid leads us to a rickety ladder by the curtain and
scales it without hesitation.

One after the next, V, me, and then Tall crawl up the
ladder and to the stage rafters. The kid is sitting on a plank
with his legs dangling over the ledge. The height doesn't
seem to bother him one bit.

He jumps to his feet and walks across the wobbly plank like it's his living room floor. None of us are ready. Especially not Tall.

"These feet were not made for that catwalk," he says.

"You'd rather stay back there in the workshop?" I ask.

He shrugs, probably thinking about that empty room with all the strange gadgets, symbols, taxidermy, and spirit cabinets. It's not the kind of place you want to be left by yourself.

"On second thought, tall guy gotta like heights, right?" he says, and takes a rung up.

"Sure, Tall. Just, be careful."

We crab-crawl our way along the first plank, past a network of walkways, ropes, and pulleys above the stage.

The kid turns to us. "Quickest way to get to the other side and to the lobby. Otherwise, you get out there and the ushers might ask us a million questions. Just don't look down."

Too Tall takes each step extra gingerly, and we keep having to pause for him to catch up.

A massive crowd stretches as far as we can see. Smoke billows up and crawls through the rafters. Pit musicians bend a saw eerily, like a haunted house. I crane my neck but can't quite see the stage from our angle.

"So what should we call you?" Veronica asks the kid.

"Lonzo, Little L, Li'l Lonz, or whatever you like," he says as he turns to us with a bright, broad smile.

"And what do you do here?" Veronica asks.

"Unofficially, I'm a magician's assistant," he says. "I help Herman out, carry things around, and some other stuff."

"And you live here?" V asks.

"I live on the road. I actually started as a stowaway. They found me in Louisville, realized they might as well put me to work." The kid laughs with a rasp, like how I imagine an old-timey train might sound. He's got this baby face, but he feels much older than us.

"Hey, y'all ever seen Black Herman's Private Graveyard trick?"

"In a way, I have," I say.

"Yeah, well, it's the best magic trick in the world."

There's a giant poster hanging over the balcony of a dark-skinned man with feathers coming out of either side of a strange hat.

"Who's that guy?" I ask.

"That's Mr. Marcus Garvey. This is his theater. People 'round here love him," the kid replies. "Oh, look down, Black Herman's about to start his last trick before intermission."

"You just told us not to look down," Tall says with a tremble in his voice.

"Well, now you can," Lonz replies.

Below, I can finally make out Black Herman at center stage. He looks younger, but not that much younger than when I met him in his private graveyard. I'm so happy to see him, I wave and almost actually say "hello." He's in his Prince Albert coat and pin-striped pants, and he's got an Echo Stone around his neck. As he talks to the crowd and moves around, I can see it even better. It looks just like the one I have, a stone in the shape of a triangle, except instead of a Watch of 13 in the center, there's a carving of a round eye.

"*The Echo Stone*," I whisper to V, and point down.

I wonder, did he carve that eye himself? Did that help him master his stone, somehow, like Long Fingers's watch?

V sees it and nods as Black Herman makes an announcement.

"Ladies and gentlemen, please welcome the marvelous mystic—Madame Debora Sapphirra."

A spotlight finds a woman at the back of the audience wearing a long flowing robe, giant gold earrings, and her hair in braids wrapped on top of her head.

Herman's voice booms from the stage.

"There are those among us who are possessed by demons. They're an ember that could start a fire."

Madame Debora moves through the audience, like she's searching for someone.

"The mystic Madame Debora knows where the demons lie," Herman booms right as a bulb pops onstage. The musicians add a wave of the saw.

Lonz nudges me. "If you want to get to the other side before intermission, we better keep moving," he says. We all snap out of it and continue edging toward the other side of the walkway, though V, Tall, and I keep peeking down.

The woman moves from aisle to aisle, holding her hands to the audience like she's warming them by a fire. There's a shriek as two men jump from their seats, screaming. They run and jump up on the stage as the whole audience nearly falls out of their chairs. The men stop cold in front of Black Herman. He holds his ground and lifts his palms. More bulbs pop, and the houselights flicker on and off.

Lonz waves us on as we continue to tiptoe, almost to the other side of the theater.

Herman pours the contents of a beaker out onto the floor and strikes a match, and a flame erupts on the stage. He holds his hands up as the two men rise and levitate above the floor. Then something long and coiling falls from the shirtsleeve of one of the men. Too Tall yelps beside me as a snake slithers onto the stage floor. Another snake pops out of the buttoned-up shirt of the other man. Half the audience is out of their seats as the snakes squirm toward Herman. He grabs them both in practiced hands and holds them toward the audience.

As he stands there with a snake in each hand, he reminds me of someone . . .

Maestro.

Maestro as Heka.

The two "possessed" men are holding steady in midair. Herman raises his hands a bit higher, and they rise a foot off the ground.

"I've never seen anything like this," V says.

"Except Maestro," I say. "At the stones of the cosmos."

Veronica nods, her expression a mix of fear and awe. "There's so much more power in magic than we ever knew."

Little Lonz taps me on the shoulder. "Trick's almost done. Here's our stop."

We're at another ladder.

The crowd goes bananas for Herman as we climb down. *If only Pop could see this,* I think.

And then I remember this is an echo and he could have visited. *Maybe he has?*

Lonz leads us into the lobby. There is a table with a Black Herman poster behind it. Some herbs and potions are piled in tiny glass vases. There's a stack of books on one side. A small sign reads *49 Cents*.

"Well, here we are," says L.

"Here? But where's"—I lean closer and whisper—"the *Missing Key*?"

"Right here," says Little L like I'm missing something obvious.

The books are copies of *Black Herman's Secrets of Magic, Mystery and Legerdemain.*

Next to that stack is a single copy of a smaller book, called *Black Herman's Missing Key to Success, Health and Happiness.*

"It—it's a book?" I stutter.

"What'd you think?" asks L.

V clears her throat extra loud. "Don't look now," she says under her breath, glancing to the auditorium doors.

But of course, I look.

And there's Maestro, striding toward the table.

He catches me staring at him.

Young Maestro, not my time's Heka-headdress-wearing Maestro, but the guy who just dropped in on my father in Georgia. Maestro, fresh and eager to master the mysteries of the Realm.

He sees me, and I freeze.

Then I remember he has no idea who I am.

He keeps walking toward the table.

But I'm closer, and I get there first.

I grab the last copy of *The Missing Key* and set it down in front of the young woman working the table.

She gives me a strange look. Her eyes are white all the way around the pupils.

I feel Maestro staring at the back of my head. He's stunned that I just took the last copy of the book.

Maybe the lady working the table notices him and that's why she's looking at me like that.

I feel like I have to explain myself.

"A copy for my pops," I say, voice cracking.

She picks up the book. "*The Missing Key*. So your pops plays the numbers?" she asks lazily.

"Uh, yeah, the numbers," I say, not sure what she's talking about.

When adults ask me questions and I don't know the answer, I just repeat what they say and that usually works.

"Just like most people. Herman's book on numbers sells better than his autobiography. At least in Harlem. All superstitions to me. But what do I know?"

I try not to make eye contact. She hands *The Missing Key* back to me.

I can feel Maestro's desire for it, like he's about to snatch it from my hands.

Then she hits me with that wide-eyed *I'm waiting* look again.

I realize I need to pay her.

"Forty-nine cents, please," she says, pointing to the sign by the books that says the price.

I didn't think this far ahead.

"You got some money, kid?" she says.

"*I'm* looking to purchase a copy," says Maestro eagerly, jingling change in his hand.

"Well, kid?" says the lady.

"Uh, right. Let me—"

I reach into my jacket pocket, searching for something, just as a reflex.

I feel, of all things, a pouch full of coins.

I recall how Crooked Eye flipped it to me after the Nets game. I open the small pouch and pull the coins out. In giant letters, one says *ONE CENT* on the back, with Lincoln on the front. There's a whole bunch of them marked 1918. *How did Crooked know?*

I dump the sack of coins out in front of the lady. She nods, impressed, and starts counting them.

"You're good, kid," she says.

I hold the book to my chest and move to hurry off.

"Hey, kid," the lady says, and I stop in my tracks, my heart sinking into my stomach.

"You paid me too much," she says, and pushes a few coins back toward me.

I fast-walk back to my crew. Maestro is behind me.

"Hey, kid," he says. He's so close I can feel the heat of his breath.

I don't turn around. V waves for me to hurry.

"Kid, I'm talking to you," he says, louder.

I reach V, Tall, and Lonzo.

"Got it," I whisper. *"Let's go."*

"Kid!" Maestro stands over us. I realize how tall and strong he seems. Not tall like my pops, but he's a grown adult and he means us nothing good. *"Listen,"* he says, his voice low and nasty. "I know you're not from this time. Look at your hair, how you kids are dressed." I check our assortment of hoodies, jeans, and kicks. "I don't know what your game is, but hand over the book. Now!"

This Maestro may be just an echo, but he's an echo of Maestro when he came for *The Missing Key*, and that Maestro will stop at nothing to get what he came for.

"Excuse me, sir, these are my friends, th-that's their book," Li'l Lonz says, stepping forward. "And you lookin' mighty out of place yourself."

"Yeah," says V, summoning courage. "What's that suit anyway, Men's Wearhouse?"

"I said, give me that book—" Maestro says, reaching for me.

Li'l Lonz holds up a hand, makes a motion sideways, and snaps his fingers.

I feel like time itself just made a little jump.

Suddenly, Maestro's back is to us.

"Let's go," Lonz whispers.

With just a gesture, Lonz made Maestro do a literal one-eighty.

Maestro looks around, confused.

When he turns back, we're at the ladder to the rafters.

The houselights are up, and the crowds are pouring into the aisles.

Lonzo leads the way over the first rafter like a tightrope walker.

"We gotta do this again?" Tall says.

"You wanna stay back there with Maestro?" I ask.

Maestro is climbing the ladder after us.

I realize that if Tall isn't too big to climb the rafters, Maestro isn't, either.

"Hurry," says V, thinking the same.

We shuffle to about the midway point, trying to help Tall keep up.

I look back, and Maestro is getting his footing on the rafters.

Then there's a cracking sound, like a tree is about to fall over.

Tall's plank is cracking.

"Guys, guys!" he says, terrified. "What do I do?"

"Slowly make your way off the plank and toward us," V tells him.

Before Tall can even take another step, the board cracks, and Tall teeters.

"He's going to fall!" says V.

Everything moves in slow motion.

V closes her eyes and holds her hands up like she did that night on the rooftop with the rock flying toward us from the sky.

Tall drops hard off the rafter.

His face contorts like he's getting sucked into deep space.

Tall is in free fall.

V reaches toward him, straining.

Then I close my eyes.

If I can crush a can, I can grab Tall's hand.

I reach my gloved hand out and imagine catching Tall.

If I can crush a can, I can grab Tall's hand.

He jerks sideways and stops midair and hangs there.

I let out a huge breath.

He's floating a good ten feet from the dark stage. No one has even noticed.

Except Maestro. He's staring at us in total shock.

Like, who are these magical little kids?

Lonzo pumps a fist. "Yeah!" he says. "Now get him up here."

I pull my arm as hard as I can, and Tall floats up toward us. Tall looks like he's seen a ghost. I pull one last time and drop him onto the plank next to us.

I slump with exhaustion. Tall puts his arms around V, who trembles with relief.

We hurry after Lonzo to the ladder that leads backstage and jet through the hallway, back to the workshop room.

Lonzo whips open the Cabinet of Souls. "In here," he says, and Tall, V, and I pile inside.

"Okay, no matter what happens, you have to hold still, and if anyone opens this door, *stay completely quiet*," Lonz says like he means it.

I nod and notice Lonzo's top button has opened up. He's wearing a purple-tinted crystal around his neck.

"A—the crystal?" I blurt.

Lonzo winks and tucks the crystal back into his shirt. "Remember. *Completely quiet.*"

He shuts the door.

It gets very dark in there.

I can hear V and Tall breathing next to me.

"Was that a crystal—like Urma's?" Tall whispers.

"*Shh,*" V shushes.

"Li'l Lonz is from the Realm?"

"Guess so," I whisper. "Now *shh*."

"Where are they?" Maestro's voice comes from outside.

"Gone out the window, sir," says Lonzo. "You just missed them."

"Oh, come on," says Maestro. "They're in here—" He wrenches open the door to the Cabinet of Souls.

There's Maestro's determined, desperate face. His eyebrows arched high as he searches.

But he doesn't see us.

We're right in front of him, as far as I can tell. And he can't see a thing.

"Where are they?" he shouts at Lonzo.

"I told you, sir. They're gone."

"Excuse me?" Another voice enters the room. I recognize it from the show just now. It's Black Herman's. "What are you doing in my dressing room?"

Maestro is caught.

"I—um, there was this young boy and his friends. They came back here and—"

"And you were chasing this young boy into my priceless Cabinet of Souls, why?"

"I—was just leaving," Maestro says, and turns back.

He pauses at the threshold of the door.

I can guess what he's thinking.

But challenging a powerful magician like Black Herman in his own dressing room is a bad idea. Maestro realizes this, I think, and keeps walking, eyeing Herman's Echo Stone all the way out.

"Lonzo, what's this nonsense?" Herman asks.

Lonzo closes the door to the cabinet, and it all goes dark again. "Dunno, boss," he says, and flicks a latch of some kind. "Maybe that guy's possessed or something."

I can't believe no one saw us the whole time the door was open.

I run my fingertips along the inside of the wood door, wondering what it's made of.

There's a symbol carved there and that's sticking out from the recessed wood, and I can trace its grooves.

Feels like a deck of cards.

Hooker's Deck, I think. *For Illusion.*

I think about how the Magician's Lost and Found has the same kind of carving on one of its four sides. Then I feel at the same space on the back of the cabinet. There's a carving of a skull.

"Tall," I whisper. "Flick on that light you found."

"Huh?"

"Please, just do it."

The light comes on.

I can see now we are surrounded by the exact same four symbols as carved into the Lost and Found box—skull, deck, pistol, and mirror.

"Um, guys, what if the portal is this Cabinet of Souls?"

"Wait, what?" says V.

"Skull," I say, pointing. "Card deck, pistol, and mirror. The four elements. Maybe this is how Black Herman jumps into echoes? The cabinet is like a massive Magician's Lost and Found."

I hear the latch flick once again from the outside.

"Lonz?" I whisper.

"Nice meeting y'all," he replies under his breath.

A blue light fills the cabinet—a much purer, brighter light than anything that old-timey bulb could muster.

"*Whoa,*" whispers Tall.

"Wait," says V. "We're not ready! Where are we even going?"

"Uh," I say, "I dunno. We got this book, *The Missing Key*, but honestly I have no clue how to use—"

"My dad," V says, and she pulls the Echo Stone from under her shirt. She turns the small hand on the watch toward the 13, the present. "My dad will know—"

The cabinet door opens. Black Herman looks right at us.

"What in Horus's name?" he cries as the blue portal light reflects off his face.

Everything blazes bright blue to white to *gone*.

THE DAYLIGHT HITS like it's a Saturday morning, too early to wake up. Shapes and colors come into focus.

We're in the back seat of a car. My face is up against a window. Big trees and sloping hills and well-kept lawns are fenced in by tall gates. There's a sign that reads WOODLAWN CEMETERY.

And we're moving.

Pretty soon, graffiti-splashed buildings, pedestrians, car horns, and freestyle music blur by outside. Between the cracked leather seats and the scratched-up plastic wall between us and the driver, I know we're in a taxicab. In the city. Only it's the biggest cab I've ever seen, with leg room where Tall's feet actually can stretch out. I take a breath of relief.

We're close to home.

We were in such a rush turning the Echo Stone, I was worried we could end up anywhere.

I catch the reflection of the driver in the rearview. His window is rolled down, his fingerless gloves grip the steering wheel, and his sunglasses are so big they cover half his face. He's blasting Bob Marley and hasn't even noticed us.

Where are we? I wonder. *And where are we going?*

Tall rubs his eyes, and Veronica is still asleep. As I learned at Nabta Playa, apparently sometimes, when echo traveling, you arrive completely asleep.

It's summertime. Kids on the corner are splashing around a fire hydrant, blasting water like a cannon into the street. The traffic is full of wide and blocky sedans, the taxicabs are canary yellow and have checkers running along the side doors, and everybody's rocking throwback gear. An el train tagged in graffiti like an NBA star's tattoo sleeves passes on the bridge above us. Nobody is on a phone.

I'm jerked out of my daydream as the cab comes to a screeching halt.

"What you kids doing in my cab?" The driver takes off his sunglasses, eyes blistering with outrage.

Veronica's awake, blinking furiously.

Tall yawns, stretching his arms out like he's enjoying

the ride. "Take it easy, my man," he says, like it's some kind of NYC interborough code phrase to get out of trouble.

"I don't know how yous managed to sneak in here, but *I don't do free rides*," the driver enunciates.

He unlocks the doors and motions for us to get out.

"Well, go on!"

A horn blares from behind. The street outside does not look familiar at all. I don't know where or when we are, only that we're not in Echo City.

"Sir, this is not what you think," I say. "It's actually really hard to explain, and you wouldn't believe me if I did. But we're lost. Please don't leave us in the streets."

"Why not? You came from the streets," he says, and opens his door.

As he gets out, the steering wheel turns on its own. The gear shifts, and the cab edges forward.

V is staring with all her focus at the steering wheel. She's waving her hand slightly, and the wheel keeps turning.

"What the Verrazano?" the driver yelps, and jumps back into the seat and puts his foot on the brake.

"Look, sir, we're really sorry to trouble you," says V in a kind voice. "Please, just drive us to Echo City, Brooklyn, and we'll be out of your hair."

"Did you just do that?" He points to the wheel. "You

trying to steal my cab? Okay, you can tell all that to the cops." He slams the door shut. The locks around us snap down like hammered nails. "Next stop, Forty-Seventh Precinct station house."

He floors the gas and yanks the steering wheel hard, sending us tumbling over one another in the back seat.

The driver mutters to himself, "Kids probably escaped from a government facility or something. I believe it, all that stuff. KGB spy programs, Manchurian Candidates, MKUltra, Area 51 aliens, telekinetic kids, why not? I believe it."

Tall pushes himself up. "We didn't make it back to *our* Echo City, did we?"

"You're catching on," V says.

"So *when* are we?" Tall asks.

I check the watch on the Echo Stone around Veronica's neck. V had tried to wind it all the way to the 13, our present time, before we portal'd out of the Cabinet of Souls. Only the small hand appears to be a few notches short of the 13.

"We are sometime before our time," I say.

"How do we get out of here?" asks Tall.

"We need a portal," I say.

"Then where would we go?" asks V.

"I don't know."

"How do we even find a portal?" she follows up.

"I don't know," I say again.

I'm getting flustered. The problems are piling up. There's Reality-Destroying Maestro in a goalpost head-dress flipping the cosmos like a coin and hurling comets at Echo City; there's a missing key that isn't even a key but a book; and we're in the wrong echo going the wrong way in the wrong borough to some random police station in New York City. I feel like I'm up to my neck in this mess, and I have no idea how to get out of it.

"We need help," I say. "We need our parents, V." I try to concentrate on the problem at hand. "We need a portal, right? That's the only way out. Then we can go to our time, talk to Long Fingers. The good news is, someone is going to open a portal. That's a fact. I mean, that's why this echo even exists. So, if anyone opened a portal in NYC back in the day . . ."

"It's most likely our dads," V says, nodding. She holds up her hand toward the steering wheel once more.

We've stopped at a traffic light. The light turns green and the driver tries to turn left, but the steering wheel fights him the other way.

V is in a state of pure focus.

"Is she doing that?" Tall whispers.

The cabdriver holds his hands off the wheel as it continues to spin. "What the?" He grabs it and tries wrestling it back.

"Sir?" V says sweetly.

The driver turns. He locks eyes with Veronica in this strange, relaxed expression. "We really need you to take us to Echo City, Brooklyn. I'm so sorry, but we're lost and we can only pay with a couple of coins. But it would be a very good thing you'd be doing, sir. You're a good person."

"Yeah?" he says. His tongue lolls to the side like a puppy dog's.

"Yes. You are a *good person*," Veronica says like a generous queen. "Good person," she adds.

The driver goes back to the wheel and turns right.

"Next stop, Echo City, Brooklyn," he says. "Sure thing. Why not? I'm a good person," he mutters to himself. "A good person."

Tall and I stare at V for five whole seconds before anyone speaks.

"What was *that*?" Tall says, but it comes out super high-pitched.

V just shrugs. "Thought it was worth a try."

"Okay, V has supercharged mind-control powers," Tall says like he's talking to himself. "Good to know."

"But, V, how did you know you could do that?"

"I guess I didn't think about it. I really don't know how this stuff works. And I didn't *control* his mind, Tall. I don't like how that sounds. I think he really is a good person. I just reminded him."

Too Tall folds his arms like he's mad about something. He gazes out his window.

"Don't be like that, Tall. I wanted to save you when you fell off the rafters, I really did."

Tall whips his head in disbelief. "Yo—did you just *read my mind*?"

"What? No!" says V. "It was obvious you were thinking that!"

"No it wasn't," I say. "I had no idea."

"I'm saying, King, it's sketchy," explains Tall. "She just went full supernatural right. And she caught a comet in the sky like a fly ball! But if *Too Tall* with his goofy self is about to drop on his neck or his back? No powers."

"Okay, not sure you can blame her for that," I say. "But, V, I feel you in my mind sometimes, too. It's like we're talking—sometimes I even *think* we're talking—but we haven't said a word. You saying you haven't noticed that?"

"Okay," says V, looking out Too Tall's window. "Tall, I really, I mean *really* tried to catch you before you fell. I don't know what happened. I have absolutely *no idea* how I caught that rock on the roof. But people's minds? People's thoughts? I can hear them more and more. King, half the time, I don't know the difference between what's being said and what I'm hearing. Like, I have to actually look at your lips to know when you're really talking. I thought it was all in my head."

"We're around all these magicians our whole lives, and no one ever teaches us how to magic," I say.

"Where we headed in Echo City, kids?" the cabdriver asks.

"Yeah," Tall says, turning to me. "Where are we going?"

Out the window, we drive pass a Loews movie theater. *Ghostbusters* is plastered on the marquee.

"Guys, I think we're in the eighties," I say.

"So that would mean our dads are teenagers?" says V.

"Where do teenagers in Brooklyn go in the eighties?" asks Tall.

"I have a guess," I say.

WE SIT AT a red-and-white-checkered tablecloth, waiting for a pepperoni pie at Not Not Ray's Pizza. Luckily, there are enough one-dollar coins in Crooked Eye's sack for a few slices, with toppings.

Most of Brooklyn is *completely* different from how it was in the eighties. But not Not Not Ray's.

When we first walked in, I thought we'd jumped back to our time. Same brick oven, same garlic knots dripping oil behind the glass, same smell of baking crust, crisping cheese, and home-roasted goodness.

Our dads weren't there when we arrived. But Tall proposed his go-to "let's eat" plan, and the vote in favor was unanimous.

As we wait for our pie, I dive into *The Missing Key*, hoping to find a clue.

"What's in that bad boy?" asks Tall.

"It's a dream book," I say, scanning the text on an open page. "Herman tells you what numbers to bet based on what you dreamed the night before, I guess."

"You're kidding," says V.

"Nope. Listen: *Climbing—If you climb a tree, you will rise to honor; if a mountain, many difficulties will confront you—42-6.*"

"That's ridiculous."

"Wait, *I* had a dream I was climbing," says Tall.

"A tree or a mountain?" I ask.

"Fire escape. Does it say fire escape?"

"Not that I see," I say.

"There must be some kind of code in there," says V.

"Maestro said this book was the key to immortality," I say. "Think that's how he discovered his Echo Stone, back in the day? By using this book?"

"But now we've got the book instead of him," says Tall.

"Echoes don't work that way," say V. "When the real Maestro went to get that book, we weren't there to stop him. It's a safe bet that he got it then."

I nod. "Sounds right to me. He probably figured out how to decode this book."

"Does it say anything about immortality?" V asks. "Like, if you dream you live forever or something?"

"Not that I see, but kinda the opposite—like, *Assassination—To dream that you are being assassinated indicates much success in business—2-00.*"

"Oh, you have got to be kidding me," says V.

"Nope. And here's another: *Ghosts—To dream you see a ghost clad in white is an omen of good fortune—7-7.*"

"We are definitely going to need my father for this one," V grumbles.

Matteo's father sets a steaming pie down at our table as the bell at the front of the door rings. *"Buon appetito,"* he says.

A group of kids storms through.

It's them.

Pops, Long Fingers, and Maestro. But they're just kids, like us.

Pops has that same smile, except he's super skinny with a Kangol hat and an Adidas shirt that's one size too big. Long Fingers stands taller without that slouch he's developed over the years. He wears a bright red tank top and some thick glasses.

I swear Pops catches me staring, but I can't look away. I wonder, *Do I look like that? Move like that?*

It's like I'm seeing double. There's the boy he was in front of me, but I can't help seeing the Pops I know in his cocky smile, the way he pokes out his chest with pride. I would never have called him cocky before, but he looks that way now.

Pops puts his arm around Maestro, who's thin in the shoulders and looks even more delicate and bird-chested.

Long Fingers sits on the table next to us, a piece of paper in his hands.

Veronica stops chewing. I'm sure she's thinking what I'm thinking. Like, *Look at these kids who become the men that raised us. Try not to let your head explode.*

Too Tall is the only one digging into the pizza.

"Alessandro!" Pops calls, and waves.

"Buongiorno, ciao, Preston," says Alessandro. "Matteo!" he calls.

A young Matteo comes out from the back, also a teenager, looking as gangly as Too Tall and wiping his hands on a rag. Matteo and his dad stare at my dad like he's about to do something cool. *I know that look.*

"Have you seen my card trick?" says Pops, and faster than a blink, he spreads his arms out to either side, and levitating playing cards fill all the space between his hands. The deck makes a crescent shape, like he's holding a rainbow of cards at either end. You'd think there must be string holding them all up and together, but there's nothing.

Matteo and Alessandro applaud and whistle. "Bravo, bravo!" they cheer.

Pops slaps his hands back together, shows them his empty palms, like there was never even a deck of cards there, and then takes a bow and sits by his brother.

"Why do you show off like that?" Long Fingers grumbles.

"My magic is for the world, *Lawrence*," he says like it's a dig. "You nag like Heyward. Or should I call you Dad? 'Cause you sound like Dad."

"Well, yeah, Heyward and Dad wouldn't like you doing magic in public like that," says teen Long Fingers.

So Grandpa Freddy and even Crooked Eye were anti-magic back then?

"Do you have money to pay for a slice? 'Cause I sure don't," says Pops. "Don't sweat it, brother-man." What he says next is so quiet I can barely make it out. "Magic tricks are a great cover for real magic."

"Don't be jealous, Long Fingers," says teen Maestro. "Just 'cause your magic skills are weak compared to Preston's."

"Marcus," says my pops. "Don't talk to my brother like that."

"Sorry. Sure thing," Maestro says cheerfully.

I lock eyes with V, wondering if she can read my thoughts. *Did my dad just order Maestro on how to talk to his brother, like some prince to an underling?*

"I'm just excited," Maestro continues. "Today's the day."

"Let's review," says Long Fingers.

I turn my neck as if I'm looking out the window and see a map in front of him.

"I got four possible sites mapped out at Woodlawn that I think could be Black Herman's unmarked grave," Long Fingers says, pointing down at the map.

"Question," says my dad, holding up a finger.

"This is not a grave-digging situation, P."

"Answered, thank you," he replies.

Maestro giggles like these two are beyond hilarious.

"If I'm interpreting this right, the Skull will present itself if we find his grave."

"I can't believe we're actually doing it," says Maestro.

"Everybody got two tokens?" asks Long Fingers.

I realize where they're going, and why we appeared in this echo where we did. I lean in and whisper to Veronica, "They're going to Woodlawn Cemetery."

"Explain," she replies, and takes a bite of her slice.

"That's where they make their portal," I whisper. "That's why we arrived at Woodlawn earlier. We always arrive in a new echo near where the portal is made."

I hear my uncle behind me say to my dad, "P? What's wrong?"

Veronica arches an eyebrow. "Um, guys. Heads up, but I think our cover is blown."

My pops is standing over our table, staring at my copy of Black Herman's *Missing Key.*

"What's this book? Did you take that from us?" he asks.

"What? No. That's mine. Why would you even ask that?" I say.

He gives me a suspicious, sideways look.

Then the book leaps off the table and flies into his hands all by itself.

He just uses magic like that?

"Long Fingers, this book one of yours?" he asks, and hands it to his brother.

Long Fingers looks it over and opens the cover. "Wow, this is an original, first edition, first printing! This book is beyond rare. How did you get it?"

But I'm stuck on his words. First edition, first printing . . .

I remember the other Maestro's words about *The*

Missing Key. The original. The very first. The later versions made changes.

The first edition—*that's important,* I realize as young Uncle Long grills me.

"Um," I say.

"Our dads are big Black Herman nerds," V jumps in.

Long Fingers seems satisfied with that. He hands the book back. "That's a real find. We're Black Herman fans, too."

My dad is still hovering, examining us from face to face.

It's beyond strange that my own father is looking at me like a stranger.

I can't take it, and I look away.

Too Tall's mouth is full, lost in the pizza sauce, but V returns his glare.

"She's in my brain," says Pops. "LF, she's in my brain! How is she in my brain?"

"Huh?" says teen Long Fingers.

Veronica holds Pop's attention. His expression relaxes. He smiles an easy smile. He looks more like himself.

"I got to sit down," says Pops. "Brother-man, you're not going to believe who these kids are."

VERONICA LEANS TO me and whispers, *"Relax."*

"The marvelous Madame Debora Sapphirra's grand-kids!" teen Pops announces.

"What? No way!" says Maestro, standing up.

"Believe it," says Pops. "She just told me *using her mind*."

"Grandma taught me everything I know," Veronica says with a shrug.

Sometimes she's a little too good at lying.

Long Fingers stands up, looking serious as a gravestone. "This is fate," he declares.

"So you have powers? Like, real powers?" Pops asks us.

"Comes and goes," says V truthfully.

"Wow, I never met anyone else like me." Pops turns to me. "You too?"

"Yeah," I say, feeling very shy. "Comes and goes."

"Like, what stuff can you do? I can make things come to me with my mind and levitate small things, like this deck."

"One time, I focused really hard and made a whole plume of smoke into the shape of my fist," I say.

"Wow," says Pops, eager eyes wide.

"He can lift me with just his mind," says Tall, slurping up a stretch of melted mozzarella. "Caught me in midair so I didn't fall."

"You must be able to get away with anything," Maestro says with envy.

"But do you know what today is? This can't be a coincidence," says Long Fingers like he's the only one who gets how important everything is.

"Yes," says V, leveling her best Madame Sapphirra gaze at this young incarnation of her dad. "Today is the day we help you find Black Herman's grave."

The three boys are floored.

"Sweet Isis on earth," says Maestro.

I detect Veronica is enjoying her role of misinformation mystic a little too much.

"V," I say, standing up. "Sidebar?"

We step outside and talk in low voices as the James brothers and Maestro watch worshipfully from the other side of the glass and Too Tall enjoys his slice.

"What happened to not messing with echoes directly?" I ask.

"That was when we had something to observe," she says. "Now we just need a portal opened. These goofballs can't help us decode *The Missing Key*. And sorry, but we don't have time for them to ride the subway through three boroughs to get up to the Bronx. So we'll give them a ride." She waves to our new friend the cabdriver, parked out front. He cheerfully waves back.

"Okay, V, this is spooky. You're, like, controlling *everyone*."

"I'm not controlling anyone!" she insists. "Everyone wants to do what they're doing. I'm just helping them along."

"But—Madame Sapphirra?"

"Come on, King, what was I supposed to do? Tell them who we really are? Please. No teenage boy is ready to meet his future children. I'm trying to mess with their brains, not break them."

"I hear that. I'm not ready to meet my teenage father. Can I ask you this, though, V—my dad—does he seem a little full of himself to you?"

She flashes a condescending smile and touches my cheek. "Wow, King. I'm proud of you. You actually observed that all on your own, without Sula or someone pointing it out."

"Not funny, V."

"Anyway, remember what your dad said?"

"What? When he told Maestro, '*Yo, don't talk to my brother like that*'?" I imitate like a goon.

"No, not that father. Your *real* father, back at the stone circle in the sands. He said to learn everything we could about Maestro. That that's the best way to beat him. So, what better way to learn than by being his younger self's friend?"

"You make a scary amount of sense sometimes, V."

TWO GENERATIONS OF James kids plus young Maestro and Too Tall pile into the checkered taxicab. I guess the driver is still under V's influence, because he's happy to take us back to the Bronx and doesn't mind the extra bodies. Tall, V, Pops, and Long Fingers cram into the back seat. V volunteers Maestro and me to take the front passenger seat together. She says we're the narrowest of everyone, and everyone agrees that we are.

I see her plan. She wants me to get to know Maestro. Or Marcus, I should say.

I have to admit, I like Marcus. He feels younger than the guys he's hanging with, like he's just trying to keep up. He's smooshed against the passenger-side window, and

I'm smooshed between him and the driver. He probably can't wait to get to Woodlawn, watching the city pass by and fantasizing about the occult legend of Black Herman.

"So, um, what you guys hoping to find at the cemetery?" I ask.

"Um, Black Herman's grave," he says, like, didn't we cover this already?

"I know. I mean, what's in there, you think?"

"Honestly? I'm hoping to find the Skull of Balsamo."

So is this when they find it? I wonder.

"Yeah? You know, I heard Black Herman did have that trick for a time."

"Yeah," he says, nodding as if impressed that I've even heard of the Skull. "Long Fingers thinks so, too. Herman was friends with this magician, Jossefy. *He* claimed he traveled two centuries into the past to the dungeons of the Inquisition. This was back in the eighteenth century, when they'd throw you in a dungeon if you did magic. Jossefy found the famous magician Count Alessandro di Cagliostro. Know who he was?"

"Wasn't he, like, an old Italian magician?" I say.

"Yes, famous for having the Echo Stone." That perks me up. "So Cagliostro, real name Joseph Balsamo, presented Jossefy with his own skull."

"That doesn't make a ton of sense, does it?"

"No, it doesn't. But that's Jossefy's story. Only, can I tell you something?"

I nod for him to go on, then realize he's waiting for me to respond out loud, like he needs hard proof I want him to keep talking. "Yes. Please, tell me something."

"I don't think it's really Balsamo's skull," he says, like he's relieved he got the green light.

I wonder, do my dad and uncle, like, not let him speak?

"Whose skull is it, then?" I ask.

"I have a theory. First," he says with a faint lisp, "why isn't it Balsamo's skull? Does that mean that Jossefy was lying? Well, I'll tell you. I actually *don't* think Jossefy was lying. Cagliostro was lying." Marcus grins and bites his lip, like he's waiting for me to say no, that's not true, that's impossible.

Instead I say, "Explain."

This makes him very happy. "Well, it comes down to two things. Whether you believe it's possible to time travel, or it's possible for a person to hand another person his own skull."

"That makes sense."

"Personally, I think it's probably possible to time travel, but not the other thing. Therefore, it was Cagliostro who's lying. Jossefy went back to the eighteenth century, and Cagliostro handed him a skull. It's just that it wasn't his own."

I think about his story from what I've learned about how the Realm really works. I realize that his logic might make sense, but he might still have it backward. You *can't* actually time travel, as far as I know. You can travel to an echo of a time loop, but that's not the same thing. You technically *could* travel to an echo and discover your own skull, however, if someone decapitated an echo of you. It's making me dizzy thinking about it.

But it's just as likely that Jossefy traveled to Cagliostro's echo, and that's how he got the skull. And who knows, maybe Cagliostro was lying?

"Well, I guess it does make some sense that Cagliostro didn't give his own skull away," I say. "I mean, it'd be hard to do anything without a skull. So whose skull is it, then?" I ask again, trying to keep Marcus talking.

"Well, Jossefy actually wrote about meeting Cagliostro in his journal, which Long Fingers got his hands on somehow. Cagliostro gave him the skull he described as belonging to himself, 'a master of four ways—from north to south, east to west.'"

Master of four ways, I think. *Or four elements.*

In other words, one who can open the way to the Realm.

"Why?" I ask. "How was he a master of four ways?"

"Well, one version is how Cagliostro traveled. He was

born in Sicily. Went south to Egypt, and east as far as India, to learn the arcane arts. Then he was a big hit up north, in London. North to south, east to west. But some say it's because his mother claimed she was descended from Charles Martel, grandfather of Charlemagne, defender of western civ or whatever, who conquered every which way. But I don't think it's any of that nonsense."

"You don't?" I ask. Now I'm really interested.

"This part maybe *is* a little complicated. Long Fingers *definitely* thinks so." He drops his voice even more, like every time he thinks about my uncle, he quiets down. "So, I'm sorta obsessed with history. Do you like history?"

"Sure," I say. And I realize I may be onto something with Marcus here. We need to find where in history Maestro wants to make the new prime reality. Maybe he's thought about this since he was a kid? "If you could travel to any point in history, when would it be?" I ask him.

"Great question—let me do you one better. What person, lost to history, could've had the biggest impact on the world, if he hadn't disappeared?"

"Um, I really couldn't say, Marcus. There's a lot of people in history. Who are you thinking of?"

"I'll give you a hint. He has the two most famous parents, like, ever."

I shrug.

"And he combines east and west, north and south."

I got nothing.

"He's Egyptian. And Roman. And Greek."

"I don't know, Marcus. Tell me."

"Ever hear of Caesarion?"

I shake my head. "Sorry, no."

"Guess I shouldn't be surprised. But he could have been famous, like, really famous, like, has-a-whole-month-named-after-him famous. Everyone has heard of the guy who took his place. That's the month of August."

"You're saying, August took Caesarion's place?" I try to clarify.

"Yup. Ever hear of Augustus, the Roman emperor? He was Julius Caesar's heir. But Caesarion, he's Caesar's son by Cleopatra."

"So Caesarion's parents were Julius Caesar and Cleopatra? I've heard of them," I say.

Marcus chuckles. "Yup. That's how he combines east, west, north, and south. East, because he's Egyptian. West, because he's also Greek. North, because Rome conquered all the way up to Britain. And south, because Egypt's in Africa."

I put some enthusiasm behind my nod.

"Caesarion vanished when Rome conquered Egypt. But you know what I think?"

"What do you think?" I ask, now that I know he means those type of questions.

"I think Caesarion lived on, discovered the Echo Stone, and became Althotas, the most powerful magician ever, and that the Skull of Balsamo is really *his* skull," he says softly with a wink and a nod.

"Okay, so how did Cagliostro get Caesarion's head?" I ask.

"Althotas was Cagliostro's mentor, who disappeared. Very mysterious. Rumored to be immortal. Once Althotas teaches Cagliostro his mystic secrets? We don't hear from him again. And Cagliostro appears with the Echo Stone. And he hands time-traveling Jossefy a human skull. So," he says, shrugging, "maybe Cagliostro killed Althotas and took his Echo Stone. And then sorta passed his head along, I guess?"

"But then why do you think Althotas is Caesarion?"

"Well, the Echo Stone makes you immortal, right? There's no historical record of what happened to Caesarion. Everybody assumes Augustus did away with him, but I don't. He was too powerful. The son of the living Isis?" Marcus says, like a worshipper. "He could have escaped. He could have cast a glamour and hidden his true appearance.

Or had a body double? Anyway, he could easily have lived until Cagliostro's time."

It hits me that Marcus may be the key to understanding Maestro. A "master of the four ways" could make a body double by replacing himself with his echo self. I mean, easier said than done, but technically possible.

I don't know about immortality or anything, but he could even pull a grown Caesarion out of his echo, and name him Althotas.

By my count, Marcus referred to three distinct time periods in this conversation alone: Jossefy in the nineteenth century, Cagliostro in the eighteenth century, and Caesarion, whenever he was. I wonder if any of those hit close to the mark.

"Hey, Marcus, if you could live forever in any time period in history, which time would it be?" I ask him.

"That's a really good question," he says. "I'd have to think about that one. I mean, I would love to visit the court of Kublai Khan. Or see who built the pyramids in China. Or whether Atlantis is real. Wait, I got it!"

"What? When?" I ask.

"On second thought, maybe not. I was thinking the Italian Renaissance, but then I realized pizza wasn't invented yet."

THE SUN SETS over the sloping green fields of Woodlawn Cemetery. We drive past the big sign out front, and it feels more like a golf course than a graveyard. Then we reach the hills studded with gravestones of all sizes, some huge and elaborate, some mausoleums, some looking like mansions. Some plots have life-size statues of great men on horseback or robed ladies with angel wings, and I wonder about those folks and their families, and whether anyone visits them anymore.

Long Fingers directs the driver according to his map.

"Did I just see a sign for Woodlawn Ossuary?" asks Too Tall from the back.

"Yeah, so?" asks V.

"Nothing, just, what's an ossuary?"

"It's where they keep dead people," grunts Long Fingers.

"Ah," says Tall, nodding. "For some reason I keep thinking of Osiris. Like, the Egyptian god. Must be all that time I spent with Long F . . ."

Long Fingers gives Too Tall a death stare.

". . . Nobody," Tall catches himself.

"Long Nobody?" asks my pops.

"Stop the car," orders Long Fingers, suddenly alert.

"Stop the car," V repeats under her breath.

The driver hits the brakes.

"Let me out," says my uncle. "Hurry, Daddy Longlegs."

"Take it easy. I got this extra equipment over here," Tall says, pointing to his knees.

Long Fingers gets out of the cab, map in hand, and rushes over to the sign for WOODLAWN OSSUARY. He then looks at his map.

"This is it. The starting point. It says, 'Begin at the old man of Egypt.' I was looking for a statue of an old Egyptian! But yes, an ossuary, like Osiris, the Egyptian god of the dead, who was also the *father*—aka the old man—of Horus, the god of kings. Black Herman, you sly dog."

Too Tall leans in and asks me, "Did I do good?"

"I think you did," I say.

"Couldn't have done it without you," Tall says to Long Fingers. "For real," he mumbles under his breath.

We trail after Long Fingers as he tracks the map.

"My, um, uncle was telling me about Horus," I say. "Since he's the god of kings, like that's supposed to mean something to me, 'cause my name is *King*."

"You should listen to your uncle," says Marcus. "Names weren't just names to ancient Egyptians. A name was, like, your essence."

"Well, my name is Kingston," I say.

"That's a cool name," says my dad.

Figures.

"Does that make me a king, or a *king's son*?" I wonder.

"Why not both, like Horus?" says Marcus. "He was king on earth. His father, Osiris, was king of the *duat*, the realm of the dead."

"Horus's father was king of the Realm?" I say in disbelief.

"The realm of the dead, yeah," says Marcus. "See, the legend goes, there was Isis and Osiris, and they were like the perfect couple. Only Set got jealous. He's the god of chaos and storms and stuff. So he built this beautiful sarcophagus and tricked Osiris into getting inside. Then

Set locked the box and threw it in the Nile and drowned him. So Isis had to resurrect Osiris, and they gave birth to Horus. So Horus went and defeated Set and became king, and Osiris returned to the realm of the dead and became king there. So all Egyptian kings were Horus on earth. When they died, they became Osiris, king in the afterlife."

"Yeah," says Too Tall. "That's the story I heard, too."

"But can I tell you something?" Marcus asks.

"Yes, Marcus, please tell me something," I say.

"There's someone whose story is *really* like Horus's."

"Who's that?" I ask.

"Guess."

"Um, can you give me a hint?" I ask.

"Okay. I just told you about him. In the car ride."

"All right, Professor O*dork*is, enough already with the history lectures," my dad butts in. "We've got some enchanted artifacts to get? Remember? Sorry about him," he says to me.

"No. It's really okay," I say with some snap behind my words.

Teen Pops shrugs. He starts shuffling a deck one-handed.

I wait for him to walk up ahead after his brother.

"It's okay, Marcus. Tell me."

"Caesarion, of course. He was the last pharaoh. The last Horus on earth. His dad was dead—and he sure was a king of kings. His mom was Cleopatra—Isis incarnate. I mean, she literally told everybody she was the living Isis. Only . . ."

Marcus pauses and gazes out on the cemetery grounds. We've reached a short peak where you can see gravestones for what feels like miles around. I picture what maybe Marcus is imagining—armies and legions of the dead beneath the earth.

"What is it, Marcus?" I prompt him, knowing how he likes that.

This time, he stays quiet.

I think about what it must have been like for a history-obsessed kid like him to discover the Realm. The thrill of jumping from echo to echo and experiencing all these places for real. And I remember back in Georgia, how Maestro told my dad all about his echo travels. How was that not enough for him? Seems like there are enough echoes to satisfy a lifetime. When did Maestro decide he had to mess with everybody's destiny?

"It's just sad, you know?" he says, so quietly I barely hear. "I mean, Horus won in the end, but Caesarion lost. His Set—Augustus—won, and that was the end of Egypt. It didn't have to be that way. And Egyptians, they believed in magic. *Real* magic. Sometimes, I imagine what the world would be like if, instead of Rome, *Egypt* founded our society. Our language, our symbols, our buildings. Then magic would be the true religion, you know?"

"Yeah," I say.

I remember Maestro as Heka at Nabta Playa—*magic is the one true religion . . .*

"A lot of harm that happened in the world—all that conquest, persecution, and slavery—I think maybe then it wouldn't have happened."

"That's a nice thought," I say.

"If Egypt didn't fall."

If Egypt didn't fall.

LONG FINGERS STANDS before a vast lake, staring at his map. The banks are dotted with gravestones all the way around, like a crown. Long Fingers has checked every marker in the area, double-checked it against his map, but seems frustrated. Every time he makes a bad guess, he growls low in his throat, a lot like he does when he's older.

"Supposed to be here," he says to himself, feet at the edge of the water.

I think about how I met Black Herman that time back at his private graveyard. *It's about reflections,* he told me. *Reflections and gates.*

I stare into the surface of the lake, scanning the way

the light plays on the faintly rippling water. I notice that some patches of water catch the light differently—with sharper edges.

Then I realize there are crystals in the water.

Our silhouettes reflect back at us. Then our shapes fade as a new image appears. A rectangular block comes to light in the depths of the water.

It's a coffin.

"Guys, look!" I say, pointing.

Everybody peers into the waves.

"What?" says Pops.

"I don't see it," says Marcus.

"Just give it time. Look," I say.

"There," says Long Fingers, flashing a bold smile.

He looks down at where he's standing, then makes a little hop and backs away.

"Okay, here goes." Long Fingers starts to chant. *"Let the earth be still, let the air be still, let the sea be still. Do not be a hindrance to this, my divination."*

Everybody is stone quiet, and I get a chill, remembering when Maestro recited his grim spell at Nabta Playa.

"Open my eyes so that you may reveal to me. Open the world to me."

As I watch the lake, a shadow forms on the banks. My

breath catches as a coffin appears before us all in the grass, over six feet long.

"Holy Houdini!" says my dad. "Long, you did it!"

"*Wow*," says Marcus.

Tall, V, and I react a little differently. More like, *okay, what now?*

The top of the wooden coffin is carved like a sarcophagus to look like Black Herman in an eternal resting pose: arms crossed over his chest, holding two rods, and wearing an Egyptian headdress. His eyes are blank.

"Wow, Black Herman was really into ancient Egypt. Almost as much as you and Professor Odorkis, huh, Long?" says Pops.

"Beautiful," Marcus says, caressing the wood and ignoring the comment. "Look at these markings."

There are straight lines running across the wood-carved Herman from head to toe.

"Very odd," says Long Fingers. "Traditional Osiris pose. Indicating that he's become Osiris, king of the dead."

Black Herman, king of the dead, I think. *Unc doesn't know how right he is.*

"But what are those lines?" Long Fingers asks.

Marcus's eyes flick up and down the sarcophagus. "There are nineteen of them," he says, chewing on his thumbnail and turning to Long Fingers. "Nineteen!"

"And?"

"In the old kingdom, they would measure the height of a king in nineteen units in reliefs and statues. It's the divine proportion of the ideal man," he says.

"Right . . . ," says Long Fingers, trying to compute the importance.

"Maybe he was trying to make sure the proportions were done in accordance with the old kingdom?" Marcus suggests.

"Could be," says Long Fingers, sounding unsure.

"Do we . . . open it?" asks my dad.

Everyone just stares at the coffin, no one daring to speak or speculate on how to open such a contraption.

"His last and greatest trick," says Long Fingers.

I think about how all those years ago, Black Herman probably went from this coffin, in the pose of Osiris, king of the dead, straight to his private graveyard. I wish we could talk to him. I mean, who better to decode his dream book than the man who wrote it himself?

Then I realize something. *They're about to open the portal, whether they mean to or not.*

Will this portal lead us to the private graveyard?

If Black Herman was "buried" here, and he ended up there . . .

When they open their portal, that will be our best chance to get out of there.

I cozy up between Veronica and Too Tall. "Follow my lead," I whisper. "When they get this thing open? Look alive, guys."

Too Tall chuckles. "Look alive, and it's a coffin," he says.

Long Fingers takes the first stab at it. "Here goes," he says, hands on the lid, which pops open without fuss.

"Wasn't expecting that," says Too Tall. "Figured we'd need a code or a key or a secret password or something."

Long Fingers gives the coffin a suspicious glare. "It just opened."

Tall covers his nose with his ball cap. "Is there a decayed dead dude in there?"

"I don't smell anything," says V.

Tall lowers his hat and shrugs. "I try to get ahead of these things."

Long Fingers reaches inside the coffin. "Only thing in this box is . . . this box," he says, and holds up the Magician's Lost and Found.

So this is how they got it?

Long Fingers, Pops, and Marcus huddle in closer and inspect the box. It has the four symbols of the elements of magic on each side, just like how I remember it. Only difference that I can tell is that there's no locking mechanism on it yet, no Watch of 13.

"Well, what's inside? Another, smaller box?" says Pops.

Uncle Long gives it a little shake. There's something solid clanging around in there.

He opens the box, and there's the Skull of Balsamo.

"There it is!" cries Maestro. "Caesarion's skull!"

"What'd I tell you about that Caesarion nonsense?" snaps Long Fingers.

But he's too enthralled with the Skull to put much behind it. He holds the Skull up to the fading sun, and its brass-lined jawbone gleams.

As Long Fingers, Marcus, and Pops are drawn like moths to the flame, I tap V and Too Tall on the shoulders.

"It's time," I say.

"What's he thinking?" Tall asks V.

"Just do what he does," V tells him.

"Hey, guys? Glad we could help you find the skull. Just wanted to say, Da—um, Preston? I think you should be nicer to Marcus. I think you're going to wish you were nicer to him when you're older."

"Wha—where are you going?" he asks, looking around and behind my back for a spaceship or something.

"Oh, and also, can I tell you something?" I say, like Marcus.

"Huh?" young Pops says, perplexed.

"I love you," I say, and jump into the open coffin.

I really just said it to see the look on his face.

V and Too Tall pile in after me.

"You're messing with his head," says V, lying on top of me.

I squeeze into a corner and make room for Tall.

"I didn't lie," I say, shrugging. "Now close the lid."

And Tall reaches his arm up, pauses to wave at our new/old friends and family, and slams the coffin lid shut.

IN THE AFTERGLOW of blue light, we arrive in Black Herman's Private Graveyard, rolling in the dewy grass. I fix my shirt, dust myself off, and have a look around.

Now, this *is a graveyard.*

Tombstones are everywhere in the blue evening glow, with shadows reaching like spirits across the moonlit ground.

"How did you know that would work?" asks V.

"At first, I thought maybe they went to Woodlawn and made a portal," I say. "But you heard them—they didn't know about the Realm and portals yet. So I thought, what if it was an accident? What if *they* opened a portal by mistake just by messing with Black Herman's coffin?"

"But how'd you get the portal to take us here?" asks Tall.

"I figured we didn't have to do a thing. If Herman faked his death, he must've used the coffin to portal to his private graveyard. So it should take us here, too. I remembered how we portal'd out of Black Herman's Cabinet of Souls, right when Li'l Lonz closed the door."

"Li'l Lonz," says Tall. "Miss that dude."

"Anyway," I say, "it was a guess."

"A good guess," says a familiar voice. "And I miss Lonzo, too."

Black Herman himself sits on a tombstone, decked out in his Prince Albert coat and evening vest. Just below a high collar and a thin tie, the pyramid-shaped Echo Stone dangles around his neck.

"Lonzo didn't stay little that long, though." Herman lights a match and takes it to the wick of a kerosene lamp that brightens a name on a tombstone.

Alonzo James.

"Good ole Alonzo. Terrible how it all happened."

"Wait—Lonzo *James*?" says V.

"Yup. Left the circuit. Settled down in Georgia, I believe, after I, well, buried myself alive. Lonzo started himself a family and everything. Had a boy named Alfred."

"Wait, *Grandpa Freddy*?" I say.

217

"You got it," Black Herman says with a wink.

"I remember Grandpa Freddy used to say he didn't even know his dad," says V.

"That's 'cause his dad had to go back where he came from," Herman adds, a note of sadness in his voice.

He pauses, looks at the ground, and rests his hand on the tombstone, like he's trying to erase a bad memory. "Wish I could offer y'all some tea or hot chocolate or something," he says. "But my little world out here, it stays pretty small."

I turn to V. "Did you know our great-grandpa's name was Alonzo?"

"I don't know, who remembers great-grand names?"

"Reginald and Angela L. Scott, Andy and Paulina Smithson, Lester and Bobbie Lee Jones, Betty and Don Stevens," Too Tall recites for us all. "Got to cherish your ancestors," he adds.

"Well said, young man. And who might you be?" asks Black Herman.

"Black Herman, this is Too Tall," I say, my mind jumbled by the realization that I hung with my great-granddad, in addition to my teenage father and uncle.

Tall stretches out and takes his hand. "I've heard a lot about you."

"Pleasure," says Black Herman. "And you must be Veronica. It's such an honor."

Veronica beams with more sincerity than I thought possible. "Why, thank you . . . An *honor*, you say?"

"And how come you know who she is, and not me?" asks Tall.

"I track all my Children of the Realm," says Black Herman.

"The crystal," I realize. "Little Lonz, remember? He wore a crystal around his neck. Like Urma."

"Like any magical being trying to exist outside the Realm," Black Herman confirms. "Lonzo was my doing. Met him after a show in Louisville. Hanging around, asking every kind of question, already figured out a lot on his own. We had to move on to the next, only he stowed away, you see, tried to come with us. But he went and stowed away in one of my magical boxes."

"Oh boy," I say.

"Yup. The real Lonzo was gone. Vanished. And I went to the Realm and tried to get him back, but I couldn't find him. Hit me pretty hard. But I did find his echo. Liked him so much and I didn't know any better, so I went and brought him home. Had that magical child help out with the shows and the road. He would get sick, like his body needed the

Realm." Black Herman shakes his head. "I had to keep that crystal around his neck at all times, since he needed the raw magic of the Realm to survive in our world."

"Like Urma." I'm trying to wrap my head around this, but V beats me to the punch.

"So that makes us . . . ," V says.

"One-eighth echo," says Too Tall.

"Is that what makes us magic?" I ask.

"The gift is fickle," says Black Herman. "But as Children of the Realm, you have extraordinary magical potential."

"But then why aren't we more messed up, like Sol?" I wonder.

"Maybe because Urma did all that Lady Dracula stuff to him as a kid," says V as she shakes in the shoulders from the thought.

"Wait, so is that why Grandpa Freddy never knew his dad?" I ask.

Black Herman nods. "Yeah, well, Lonzo had to go back to the Realm once he had Freddy. Was a very sad time. There was so much about the Realm we didn't know back then. Found out the hard way that when an echo person comes into the real world, having kids can be a serious problem."

"Why is that?" asks V. "What's the big deal?"

"When an echo of an individual comes into our reality, they act like a sponge for any trace of Realm energy. They're created to exist in a world of pure magic. So in our world, they consume without thinking, just to survive. A charged Realm crystal can satisfy them, sure. But if a child comes into the world, made from their same source? They will feed off the child." He shakes his head. "Very sad. Luckily, we figured it out early, with your grandfather. I noticed that Lonzo had stopped draining the crystals he wore. He was draining his newborn son, and the boy Alfred was getting weaker each day. Sending Lonzo back to the Realm was one of the hardest things I've had to do."

"The Realm takes everybody's dad," I say.

"It's the source of our power," says Herman, "and a lot of our pain."

"I don't recall anything about Grandpa Freddy being magic," says V.

"Your grandpa wasn't interested in magic," says Black Herman. "Otherwise, he may have awoke his potential."

"He probably wanted nothing to do with magic after what it did to his dad," I say.

Sorta like Ma, I think.

The thought makes me miss her.

"So why is it our magic works sometimes, but not always?" I ask.

"Only machines work all the time. And even those only work until they break. There's a reason magic is considered a performance art these days. Because it must be performed, each time. You must summon your creative power and potential; you must reach into your best selves, each and every time. Nobody does that always," he says, shrugging. "But we are going to need your best selves, each of you, if we're going to set the world back right."

"So you know about that, too, huh?" I say. "You know about Maestro?"

"Indeed, I know Marcus many times over."

I have a hard time squaring the young Marcus I met with the Maestro in the headdress, the one who is trying to destroy our world. But outside the Realm, they are one and the same. I have to remember that.

"I met Marcus as a teenager," I say. "I liked him."

"It's okay to like him, then and now, but not like what he's doing."

"He thinks he's going to swap our world for a better one. But he doesn't care if he destroys our world to do that," I say.

Black Herman nods. "But if you know him, you can stop him."

"That's what my dad said," I say.

"He would know. The child is the father of the man," Black Herman says.

"Wait, what's that mean?" asks Too Tall.

"Think about it some more," says V.

"But—"

"Even more," she cuts him off.

"He means, know Marcus and you know Maestro," I say. "Because Maestro came from Marcus. Okay, Black Herman. I think I know where Maestro went, but I need your help. You know how to work these stones." I take the chain from around V's neck and hold out the Echo Stone with the setting of the Watch of 13 to Black Herman. "Where on this watch would we find the echo for the fall of Egypt?"

He chuckles. "Very good, young King, very wise."

Black Herman looks to his own Echo Stone, now glowing against his chest, like the answer to every question in the universe is in there. Then he reaches for the Watch of 13 and adjusts the small hand directly to the 7.

"I suggest you not wait," he says, making a rectangle shape in the air. A vivid blue light fills it, forming a portal.

"H-how did you *do* that?" I ask.

"The Echo Stone masters the Realm, and I have mastered my stone," he says.

"So you could see into any echo?" I ask, thinking of my pops and how many times I wished I could see where he was or step into his world, even just for a visit. "You could visit any echo you wanted?"

"With this?" He gestures to his own stone. "Yes."

"So we could do that?" I ask. "If we master this?" I gesture to the stone in my hand, thinking, *Maybe, when this is all over, I'll be able to get him home . . .*

"That is a mere copy, magician, not a true stone. To express mastery of the Realm, you need to discover your own stone."

A strong wind rattles the trees behind me and chills my invisible hand. I turn and see that the bluish glow of the horizon is fading to black.

"The turn of the Realm is already happening," Herman says. "Your time is now, young King." He places a hand on my shoulder and then places his other hand on Veronica's. "And yours, young queen."

He flashes a bright smile at both of us.

"Thank you, Black Herman. I wish we could stay longer," I say.

"Don't wish too hard. Trust me. Feels like I've spent an eternity here. Staying too long can get rather tiresome."

"And you're sure you can't leave?" asks V.

"I could, but I would not last very long. My stone only keeps me alive so long as I'm here. In this place that I made with my stone. So long as I stay in this echo and wear this Echo Stone, I cannot age and I cannot die. If I were to take it off, or leave?" he says, and shrugs. "Well, I'm not entirely certain what would happen. But I'm over one hundred and thirty years old, so I don't think I'd survive very long." He gazes at the tombstones. "I was honoring those who came before me. Now I wish I'd made an amusement park."

Tall and V laugh. I try not to.

I say, "Maestro wants to be immortal *and* have time keep moving forward."

"And destroy our reality while he's at it," adds V.

"And this is unacceptable," Black Herman says. "This is why you must go, and hurry."

"You guys ready?" I nod to V and Tall.

"Yup," says Tall. "Thanks, Mr. Black. I don't do graveyards, but I like this one."

Tall then stops and turns back to Black Herman. "Oh, hey, Mr. Black. Dying to ask you. Can you explain this book to us? *The Missing Key*? You wrote the thing. Got a cheat sheet or something?"

"Ha, there is no shortcut," he says. "The key is just a

guide. You must discover the secrets within you to find the stone."

"Ah, well, I hate spoilers anyway." Too Tall pulls his hoodie over his head.

"Man, know thyself, and thou will know the universe and the gods," Black Herman says in a soft whisper that carries with the wind.

I recite the words in my head, trying to commit them to memory. *Maybe a clue?*

"I'll never get used to this," Tall says as the three of us stack hands like a team before game time and step into the glowing blue rectangle.

WE ARRIVE IN the lap of a giant statue of a pharaoh.

The statue takes it well. No knocking the easygoing smile off that dude's face.

Veronica and I land entangled, the heel of my foot somehow trapped between ankles. The statue's massive stone arms are on either side, hands resting on his knees.

There's an identical statue across from us, where Too Tall landed. His lanky limbs are splayed like a trapped spider in the massive stone lap.

"Well, at least these guys are sitting," says Tall, getting his bearings. "If they were standing, we would've landed even harder."

I peek out at the floor below.

It's a long way down.

The statue sits on a throne on top of a large stone block. The floor is at least fifteen feet away.

Veronica tries to climb, but the knees are carved smooth and she can't get a grip.

"Tall, please tell me you're having an easier time," she says, clinging with both hands to the statue's forearms.

"Hard for me, too," he says, holding on to his statue by the wrist and inching along the calf muscle. "This guy's got great skin. Don't you, Ramses? I'll call him Ramses the Lap, he looks like a Ramses."

"What's mine called?" I ask.

"Also Ramses the Lap," Tall says.

He reaches the platform mount and lowers himself to the ground from there, and helps us down.

When I reach the floor, I have a look around. I'm amazed by the sheer size and scale of this place. The two sitting statues face an open rectangular area surrounded by columns and statues on either side. The columns are painted in patterns of green and deep red, almost like palm trees. The statues wear tall, cone-shaped crowns, and a goat's beard on the chin, and some have the royal headdress with the cobra uraeus, like the sitting Ramseses. There are maybe thirty statues all around us. They stand taller than basketball hoops and all have one thing in common—one foot is stepping forward, toward the center.

"Wow, these guys are really putting their best foot f—" Tall wilts under V's stare. "I'll be quiet."

"Practice this, Tall—*think* a thing first, and then *decide* whether to say it," she instructs him.

Hieroglyphs and symbols cover every possible surface. There are gods in funky headdresses in profile, carved and painted in bold, stiff lines on every column and every wall. There's so much going on, so many bodies in motion and signs and messages, it's like being in Grand Central Station at rush hour, but frozen still. I'm overwhelmed by the size and activity, but somehow there's an order, a balance, like everything is exactly where it's supposed to be.

Except us.

Me in my blue jeans, Tall in his Jays, V with her Chucks.

The statues look like athletes, bare chests and legs, with just a covering around the waist.

I hear murmurs on ancient winds.

People coming. Their voices carry around a corner.

"*People are coming,*" V says, hearing them, too. We duck behind the back leg of one of the statues.

Not a great hiding spot, but no chance to change our minds.

On the far side of the enclosure with the columns and statues are two of the biggest slabs of stone I've ever seen, each at least a hundred feet high, separated by an archway that seems to be the entrance from the outside. Many voices chant from that direction. But the people we hear come from the other direction, deeper within the building complex.

"Is your temple how you remember it?" says a very familiar voice.

"Like it hasn't changed a day," says the voice of a woman. "Just like my tomorrow."

Is that . . . *English*?

Okay, either that's English or I can understand ancient Egyptian.

"If it works like the other echoes? You won't remember a thing."

Wait, that voice . . . *Is that . . . Long Fingers?*

V looks as shocked as I feel.

"Sorry if I'm not jumping for joy," says the woman.

"But you'll meet me again. And it will be like the first time. What couple doesn't wish they could fall in love like the beginning? You get to forget how much I annoy you," says the voice that sounds like Long Fingers, but a hundred times sweeter.

"That's a perk, yes, I understand that. But I don't love only you, Lar. I love *her*."

Veronica James shatters before my eyes.

"I love her more than anything."

It all seems to hit her at once.

She's a step ahead of me, because I only figure it out when I see her lip tremble, her eyes water, and her shoulders shake.

"And you being near her hurts her," says Long Fingers. "The truth isn't kind."

"If only we had known . . ."

"There's too many secrets with all these magicians. Too many initiations and too few revelations. If they hadn't been so tight-lipped about what happened to my granddad, maybe it'd have been different." He huffs in anger, like it's not the first time his family didn't tell him something important.

"But then we wouldn't have sweet Veronica," her mom says.

When she says that, V loses it bad, her sob so loud I'm surprised her parents don't hear.

"So we don't change a thing," Long Fingers says like he means it. "You stay here, count down, and wait until we meet again. See if you fall for that line a second time."

"Look, you appeared in a temple from out of the duat like a god. Of course I fell for it—I'm, like, he's leading me to the celestial Field of Reeds. I was just surprised there were so many taxicabs in the Field of Reeds."

"And your life will begin again, and you'll meet me again for the first time," says Uncle Long.

"I love you," she whispers.

"I love you."

"Take care of her. Please. Now go. Go now, let me make my peace."

Tall and I each have one hand on Veronica's shoulders as she hugs her elbows to her body.

My uncle's footsteps carry him deeper into the temple, the way they came, and V's mom steps into the light from the entrance, alone.

She's holding herself, similar to how Veronica is holding herself, and quietly sobbing. She wears white robes, a leopard print around her shoulders, and is barefoot. Her braids fall to her shoulders, held in place by a small circlet.

Before I can stop her, Veronica slides away from Tall and me.

"Um . . . Hi."

V's mom turns to her with a start.

"Child, you scared me."

She looks her teenage daughter up and down. Kicks, sweatshirt . . .

"You're from the duat," she says.

"You mean Brooklyn?" asks V.

"Yes, Brooklyn."

So Uncle Long Fingers brought a bona fide ancient Egyptian priestess back to Brooklyn from the Realm. Taught her the language, had Veronica, and then had to bring her back to the Realm, I guess to make sure V wouldn't end up like Sol. And apparently, this happened in my family before, and my great-grandfather Lonzo had to return to the Realm as well.

All things wondrous and magical come from the Realm, it seems.

Also, everything that ever hurt my family.

Tall flashes his best nice-to-meet-you smile and steps toward them, but I grab his wrist.

"What? Let's say hi," he whispers.

"Let's give them a moment together first."

"So this is going to sound really strange," Veronica says to her mom. "And I can tell you've already had a really strange day. Like, a lifetime in a day. And, well, I don't mean to make that worse, but . . ."

"Veronica?" says her mom. "I-is that you?"

I can just hear a breath escape V before her mom takes her in her arms.

"I don't understand it at all," says her mom. "But who else could you be, with those eyes looking exactly like my own mother's?"

They hold each other for a few solid heartbeats, and V sniffs back tears. Then the embrace relaxes, and V and her mom hold hands and stare at each other.

"You're from here? From Egypt?" asks V. "Obvious question." She snorts.

"Well, we never called it that word, but yes. I know what you mean. We call it Kemet. Your father visited me here and took me with him to the duat. He insists it was called Brooklyn, but it was the duat, which houses the rolling Field of Reeds. I had you, and it was paradise."

"I—I know. You made me sick, I guess?"

She nods. "I learned that was because I'm not of your father's world."

"I . . . never knew."

"I wish that he had told you, but I guess he was too heartbroken to try. Still, that's no excuse. My girl, you look like my mother and your father's father."

"Really? I look like your mom?"

"The shape of your mouth—"

"It's different from my dad's family."

"Because it's mine."

"Can I ask you a really bizarre question?"

"Of course."

"What's your name?"

"Neferet," says V's mom. I can hear the smile in her voice.

"Neferet. It's beautiful. You're beautiful," says V.

The chanting from outside the entrance gets closer and closer. A loud voice rises above the rest, like a trumpet making some sort of proclamation.

"Strange," says Neferet.

She listens closer to the thundering, ancient language, and goes to look out the entrance to the temple.

"I—I don't know what's brought this on," says Neferet, returning to V. "A man says he's here to consecrate the crowning of the king. This temple—Ipet Resyt—was once a very sacred place dedicated to the rejuvenation of the king. Even Alexander claimed he was crowned here. But it hasn't been used that way in centuries, since the days of the old kingdom. The man leading the royal party—he claims to be Heka incarnate on earth, and he wears the headdress of Heka."

MAESTRO.

We've found him.

Too Tall extends a fist for a dap. I lay one on him, but I'm conflicted.

I feel like the small dog chasing cars in the street. I always wondered, *What would the dog do if he ever caught a car?*

Answer: *Not much.*

Neferet looks very confused by everything going on. With Long Fingers returning her home and meeting V, she's had quite a day. And now on top of everything, Maestro is messing with her world.

However, she seems to process what's going on faster

than we do. "You had better hide deeper in the temple," she tells Veronica.

"My friends are here, too," she says.

Tall and I finally step forward.

"Well, hello."

"Nice to meet you," I say. "I'm V-Veronica's cousin. Preston's son."

"It's very nice to meet you all. You must hide, too," she says. "Be careful you are not seen. No one is allowed in the deep parts of the temple, no one but priests and gods. Punishments in these times are, well, horrific, compared with what you're used to in Brooklyn. Dismemberment is very popular."

I nod, believing her every word.

"The procession is coming, so hide well. I'm the priestess of the temple. I must welcome the royal party," she says with an exasperated sigh that sounds like she learned it from Long Fingers. "And fulfill some 'official priestess duties' I once thought I was done with. Now apparently I'll be performing them for eternity."

V, Tall, and I hurry farther into the temple.

"V, that was amazing," I say.

She nods, choked up. She needs a minute.

I lay a hand on her shoulder as we enter a narrower

hall with columns big like they were meant for a species of human who are about twenty feet tall.

I notice my hand is glowing faintly beneath my glove. Maybe it's the animal head gods or the walls loaded with mystic symbols or the incense burning in the temple, or maybe it's just ancient Egypt, but I've felt a surge of magic since we got here. I take off my glove, and my hand isn't quite invisible—it's glowing blue, the way it does when my telekinetic magic is actually working.

"My magic feels stronger in this place," I say. "Do you feel it, too, V?"

"I'm feeling so many things, King, I'm really not sure what's what."

"Yeah. Been a lot to take in."

She nods as if in a daze.

And I could really use her help.

"Anybody got feelings or ideas about what to do about Maestro?" asks Tall. "Pretty sure he's just a couple rooms away, and pretty sure he's just as superpowered as last time we saw him."

"Last time we saw him, he was Marcus. He was a teenager and wouldn't hurt a fly," I say.

"Could we maybe stop that guy, instead?" says Tall.

"What is he even doing, with this whole crowning

ceremony?" I wonder. "Why doesn't he just perform the cosmos ritual and leave?"

"Yeah, and is he, like, with the royal family right now?" asks Tall.

"I mean, Neferet said they're crowning the young king. That's got to be Caesarion," I say. "Pretty sure Marcus said he was the last king of Egypt. So yeah. How'd he do that?"

"Magic," says V, and I can't tell if she's spooky serious or just deadpan.

Voices and footsteps from the procession follow us from the corridor.

"They're coming," whispers Tall, and we hurry ahead to the next chamber.

The structure opens into a courtyard, with rows of columns making a square. The stars are bright in the night sky.

"Neferet said, hide well," I say, and look up to the top of one of the columns, at the corner of a block of sandstone. It seems so far away, but for some reason, I also feel like I could reach it.

Without thinking too much about it, I try.

I hold my hand out to the highest stone, and imagine bringing it to me.

I think of all the times I've called things to me in the past.

I think of how my dad made Black Herman's book fly to his hand.

There's a rush of air.

And the top of the column comes—

Or do I go to it?

"Did you just fly?" says Too Tall's astonished whisper from below.

I'm on top of the column, holding the highest stone.

Down on the ground, Tall and V are looking up at me, standing on top of a column. They don't seem too sure what just happened. There are carved vines and snakes and alligators tooled into the columns surrounding them, like they're down in a dangerous pit.

Did I fly? No. But by focusing on that stone, I pulled myself to it.

I wave for them to come up after me.

They look at me like I've lost my mind.

Fair point.

So I reach with my hand and focus on bringing them up to me.

My hand is glowing a more intense blue than I've ever seen. *My power—it's working.*

I concentrate on holding V's hand. Just her hand, like how I concentrated on the stone.

She flies up to me, her hand gripping mine. I help her to sit beside me on top of the column.

"Well, that was kinda fun," she says, catching her breath.

Now it's Tall's turn. I think he'll be harder, since he's bigger, but maybe because I know I can do it now, it isn't hard. It's like he's just going up for a layup, but when he gets to the basket, he just keeps going, until he reaches my hand.

"That was absolutely amazing," he whispers, pumping his fist.

From the top of the temple, we can see the Nile, and the whole ancient city. Barges drift lazily in the water. The ceremony below must be a big deal, because throngs of people as far as I can see fill the sphinx-lined walkway leading up to the temple.

The royal procession enters the courtyard just below us. Maestro leads the way in his Heka getup. He holds two staves shaped like snakes. The boy of the hour follows behind him. He's wearing the whole pharaoh getup with the headdress. Caesarion, I guess, being crowned king of kings. I think about him. I wonder, does he know how many hopes he's carrying? How does he feel about all this pressure? Does he ever want to just run away?

Maestro thinks this young king can change the world.

Only, is he sure?

I mean, it's a lot to gamble on a kid.

I'm sure he visited this echo lots. That's probably how he got in good with the royals.

Wait, I realize, *does that mean Cleopatra is somewhere with them?*

Don't get carried away chasing echoes, I tell myself. *Think. Why is he doing this?*

"He needs to be sure he can control him," I say as the thought occurs to me.

"What's that?" says Tall.

"That's why he's crowning him here. This temple means something to Maestro. Remember what Neferet said: This temple used to crown kings."

V nods. "The real king will be Maestro."

"He won't reset the echo until he knows he's in total command. He thinks he's a god. Like those old-world gods that try to control everything."

I remember what Long Fingers said about when a magician merges consciousness with the Echo Stone. *The stone is still an entity of the Realm, and the Realm is too enormous, too cosmic for any one individual. Trying to get your mind around all of it could drive a magician down a dangerous path.*

I spot the Echo Stone hooked to Maestro's belt, dangling like a talisman.

"We need to get that away from him," I whisper. "The Echo Stone that's causing all this."

"Pick his pocket, King," whispers Tall.

"Wait," says V. "You can't let anyone see. They think he's a god, and these people have, like, armies. Plus, maybe he's still dangerous, even without it?"

"Guys, if we die in the Realm, do we come back and die again for eternity?" wonders Tall.

This makes me think.

I pull the chain from my Echo Stone, just like Dad did. I gather up all the links in my hands, cup them and shake them, the whole time thinking about *the handcuffs, the handcuffs . . .* And I visualize them, just how they looked when Dad held them up to me.

I open my hands, and the chain is now shaped like cuffs.

Tall mimes applause.

The ceremony proceeds to the next room that's covered. We follow along the roof, listening for the chanting below the heavy sandstone. Up ahead, there's another, smaller room with no roof. There's an altar down there.

We wait through more chanting and incense burning.

Eventually, two figures appear at the altar—Maestro and the young king.

Heka and Pharaoh.

"Now's our chance," says V. "It's just those two."

I nod and hold out my hand, and focus.

Echo Stone.

I catch a glimpse of it on Maestro's belt and keep that image in my mind as I close my eyes. When I open them, the Echo Stone is coming toward me.

It's levitating midway between my hand and the altar.

"You got it," whispers Tall.

Suddenly, there's another body next to me.

It's a boy, arm covered in etchings of symbols, reaching his hand over my hand.

The Echo Stone slaps into his grip as he falls and knocks me over.

Then I feel a force pinning me to the sandstone.

Maestro appears, standing over me.

"I can't move!" Tall shouts, but I can't see him.

"Me neither," I hear Veronica say.

The boy, bare chested, hieroglyphs all over his body, hands the stone back to Maestro.

I don't believe what I'm seeing.

"Marcus?"

I'M ON MY back by the edge of the sandstone block overlooking the altar. Somehow, Maestro is down there, administering the rites to the boy king. He's also standing above me. Marcus is beside him. He's wearing the same headdress as Caesarion below.

What is going on?

"Really, Marcus?" says Too Tall.

Marcus looks like he's in a trance. He glances down to the altar below.

Either something is wrong with my eyes, or Maestro and Marcus are *also* beside the altar.

There are two sets of them.

One pair up here.

Another pair down there.

Only down there, Marcus's image flickers in and out like a bad connection, and every time he glitches, young Caesarion appears in his place.

Wait, I think. *Maestro is crowning . . . himself?*

How does that make any sense?

"Marcus, why?" For a moment, I wonder if he's really the Marcus I met. But he blinks like he hears me and remembers our conversation about Caesarion and all the rest.

"He said he'd make me king," says Marcus.

"Maestro, did you really kidnap an echo of your younger self so you could crown him king of Egypt and Rome in the ancient world?" V asks.

"All of my past selves may serve the glory we have become," says Maestro-as-Heka. "Who better than the boy who dreamed all of this to begin with?"

I follow his gaze down to the altar. There he crowns young Marcus to the known old world as heir to east and west, north and south.

Now, with his young self crowned, he can safely reset this echo to be the new ongoing reality . . .

Maestro-as-Heka stoops and picks up the other Echo

Stone I dropped on the roof. The copy Echo Stone, with the Watch of 13.

"Ingenious," he says as he plucks the watch off the Echo Stone. "My compliments to your father," Maestro says to V, and drops the watch back on the roof.

Her father, I think. *Is there any chance young Long Fingers is still here? Any chance he might save us?*

He holds up each stone in each hand.

"I'm going to keep this," he says, meaning the copy Echo Stone he took from me. "You won't be able to return to your time without it. You are welcome to stay here. When I am done with what I must do, time will march forward from this moment."

"You'll kill everyone we know, you monster!" I say.

"A monster, me? No, they will all live again. In my new world."

"In two thousand years?" I say. "There's no way you could know that."

"And you should count yourselves fortunate to have made it here. Now, if you don't mind . . ."

Maestro and Marcus vanish like sand in the wind.

Suddenly, the pair below look clearer and full of color.

The ancient chanting continues as the procession moves deeper into the chamber.

And then that sound goes away too, leaving us alone on the roof, fixed to the sandstone blocks, with no choice but to stargaze.

WHEN I'M ABLE to move again, I know Maestro must be gone.

In the distance, the sky blazes with lights like a cosmic firework show.

We saw something similar at Nabta Playa.

Maestro reset the echo. He must be gone by now.

I don't even feel that surge of magic from the temple anymore. I only feel how bad we just got our butts kicked.

Tall, V, and I rise like old folks with aches in our joints. I pick up the Watch of 13. The big hand has passed the 11. *Less than two hours to go.*

"Well, V—pretty amazing how you met your mom. At least we know someone here," I say. "I think the language is going to be pretty tough to learn."

"You're giving up?" she asks.

"That's not like you, King," says Tall.

"Well, let's review everything we know about echoes. There's a portal in each echo, right? So there's a portal, or there will be a portal here, somewhere, fine. And where does that portal lead? Into the last echo that was made. How do we jump through all the echoes to get back to our Brooklyn? *I have no idea.* The Echo Stone was the only way. And that's gone. You can say I'm giving up. Or you can accept that we lost."

"Nice pep talk, Coach," says Tall.

I slump back down.

"There has to be a way," says V. "This echo—it's important, and not just because Maestro chose it as the new prime. This echo was important to Black Herman, remember?"

Chin to my chest, I'm lost in the grainy details of the sandstone. I barely hear what she's saying.

"King, listen to me!" she insists. "I know it's fun to beat yourself up, 'cause you're a failure and you let your dad down or whatever, and trust me, I'm more than happy to join in once this is all over. But we need you now. We need to think. Herman *knew* what echo Maestro chose. He knew exactly how to get here. Why is that?"

"Because . . ."

"We were trying to find Maestro in one echo out of all these echoes. We found out that he was tracing Black

Herman's steps. Because he *did* follow Black Herman. He followed him here."

"Herman's *Missing Key*," I say, getting where she's going.

"But we stopped him from getting that, I thought," says Tall.

"Echoes don't work like that. We've been over this," says V. "We did not time travel. We stopped an echo of Maestro. The real Maestro got the book. And came back here. And he must have gotten the stone then, too."

"Exactly. That's when he began to change. How Sula said he spent all that time looking at his stone. This has to be the spot where he got it. Herman all but said it was. In the book," I say.

Tall whips it up from his back pocket. "Oh, you mean this book?"

The three of us huddle around the thin paperback, going through each page with our heads practically touching.

"Okay, we know it's in code, and we know it won't be obvious," I say. "It could even be something so small that it was changed in later editions. The first edition, first printing thing was important. Look for any mention of immortality, everlasting life, Egypt, temples . . . statues, maybe?"

"How 'bout 'altar'?" says Tall. *"Altar—this is no sign of marriage. If there are candles on it, this presages illness—26-7.* There's an altar down there, right?"

"I dunno, Tall . . . ," I say.

"Okay, how 'bout this. *Snakes—To dream that a snake is in the grass, beware of enemies. Dream a cobra and you are set for life—19."*

I stare at the words.

"Not sure I get it," I say.

"Yeah, I mean, there are a mess of snakes made of stone down there," says V. "But what do we do with that?"

"I mean this line," says Tall. *"Set for life.* Doesn't that sound like everlasting life or something?"

"Could be," I say.

"And a cobra? What's more Egyptian than a cobra? Those things are everywhere."

"Okay . . ."

"And usually," Tall continues, "he lists at least two numbers. This time it's just—"

"The number 19," says V. "Why does that number sound familiar?"

"We just heard it," I say. "In Woodlawn. Remember,

Black Herman's coffin? It had those lines across Herman. From head to toe. Marcus said that was how the *old kingdom Egyptians* measured the height of a king in reliefs and statues. In units of nineteen."

"Old kingdom," says Tall. "That's important, right? That's when they crowned kings here."

"Marcus said it's the divine proportion of the ideal man," I say. Mentioning Marcus gives me a sour taste.

"Well, that sorta sounds like something, I guess," says V.

"Oh, here," says Tall, flipping through the alphabetical list of dream imagery.

"What is it?" V chirps.

"*Knees.* I was wondering about knees. Had a dream about my knees, and I sorta scraped the right one on the way up this column here."

"Tall, it's not a real dream book," says V.

"It could be," he says. "*Knee—Broken knees, poverty; bent knees signify sickness; to dream of falling on the knees denotes misfortune in business; a seated knee means a great coming-together is afoot—5.25, 6.*"

"Wait, Tall, does that really say 5.25?" I say.

"Um, yes?" He squints closely at the text. "The ink seems sorta smudged, but yeah."

"Let me see that." I take the page in hand.

Tall didn't lie.

"This is a numbers book. Like, what numbers to bet based on what you dream, correct?" I say.

"Far as I know," says V.

"So how is it there's a decimal? You can't bet on a fraction. Are there any other *fractions* in that book, Tall?"

Tall thumbs through. "Not that I see."

"What could that mean?" asks V.

"Strange. Tall, any other *body parts* you see there?"

"Umm . . . Okay, here's one for *Barefoot—To dream you are barefoot means you must take a step past the first threshold—1.*"

"Okay, the feet are a number 1. You guys notice there's only one number for the body parts? Any others?" I say.

"*Head—to dream that you are suffering from a severe headache denotes you are in danger—18.*"

"Head is 18, okay, interesting," I say.

"Here's one for voice, does that count? *Voice—if you dream you've lost your voice, speak your true name when you wake—16.*"

"Huh, 16," I repeat, my hand reflexively touching my throat as I speak.

"What are you thinking?" asks V.

I'm remembering Black Herman's words back at the graveyard. *"Man, know thyself,"* I recite.

"Or how about, out of respect for gender, we just say *Know thyself,*" says V.

"Fair enough. *'Know thyself, and thou will know the universe and the gods.'* But wait, V—what if the *man* part is important?"

"Of course you would say that."

"No, not like that. I mean, like, *knowing* the proportions of *a human*: 1–19, just like on his coffin."

"Okay, but what's that got to do with this temple?" asks V.

"I don't know. But he said the temple is a puzzle. And to know thyself."

"This temple is for crowning kings, right?" says Tall. "For the Egyptians, weren't kings like gods?"

"Know thyself," I say, thinking. "Know the gods . . . And remember the procession? The king is crowned after going through each chamber in the temple."

"And what does that have to do with knees being a decimal?" asks V.

"The knees!" It hits me. "Guys, remember—where we landed—"

"Ramses the Lap?" asks Tall.

"Yes, Ramses the Lap—seated, with his hands on his *knees*," I say. "Tall, what's the entry for knees again? Just the last part, about a seated knee."

"*Seated knee means a great coming-together is afoot—5.25, 6.*"

"There's 5.25," I say, pointing to the lowest point of Tall's knee so V can see. "And 6." I point to the top of the knee. "Look, man is nineteen units. One is the foot. Eighteen is the head. The knee joint—it's 5.25–6, not quite a whole unit. That's why it's a fraction."

"And *a great coming-together is afoot*," says V, catching on. "Is that a pun? About the previous room, where all those ginormous statues have one foot forward?"

"Puns weren't just puns to ancient Egyptians," I say, remembering something someone once said.

"The temple *is* a man," says Veronica, a smile dawning.

"Race you to the feet," I say.

THE STARS ARE bright above the ancient city, and the river is calm. The torches that line the avenue of the sphinxes are faded to twinkles.

I lower Tall to the bottom first. It's kind of like lowering a fishing rod with a six-foot-five sea bass on the other end. Lowering V next is that much easier. Then I have to really concentrate on resisting gravity as it tries to slam me into the temple floor. Tall has to catch me, in the end. It's awkward. But I guess I sorta lightweight flew. Or glided, anyway.

We go to the temple entrance and gaze up at the two enormous stone blocks. Tall says, from his Long Fingers lessons, they're called pylons. Through the entrance between the massive pylons, I can see the courtyard of foot-forward statues.

"Okay, so these temples are all about the individual," I say. "One of us should play the role."

"You mean the king?" asks Tall. "I nominate King."

"Seconded," says V. "This is your show, cuzzo."

"Okay . . . Tall, what's that barefoot entry say again?" I ask.

"To dream you are barefoot means you must take a step past the first threshold," Tall recites.

"Here goes," I say, and I take my shoes off and hand them to Tall. Then I take a big step into the temple.

"Feel anything?" asks Tall.

"Well, no. But I'm not sure I'm supposed to. Let's keep going."

We go through the courtyard and up to the two seated Ramses.

"A great coming-together is afoot," says V, pondering the Ramses to her right and the Ramses to her left. "What's that mean?"

"It's a union," says a voice from behind us.

"M—N-Neferet!" says V, stumbling on whether to call her *Mom* or by her name.

Holding a torch, Neferet smiles at V. "Please, call me Mom, Veronica."

I'm struck by how much V resembles her. There's the upper lip, slightly larger than the lower, and curved in a cupid's bow. Also a wiry strength they both have—you can see it in their shoulders, in how they breathe.

She and V embrace. "I came back to get you," says Neferet. "We're lucky the high priest isn't here right now. You might lose a hand or a foot, depending on what chamber they catch you in."

"Thanks. I've got an invisible hand. That's enough for me," I say.

"You . . . you do."

I hold up my glowing hand so she can see. I hadn't thought to put my glove back on from earlier. Didn't seem to matter anymore.

"It's kinda glowy, since I've been in Egypt."

Neferet makes a face like she's impressed, but it's not the most outlandish thing she's seen. "You're gifted in magic, like your father."

"Um . . . *Mom*," V says with an awkward smile. "We . . . we actually need to get back to our time. There's a very bad man who's trying to hurt the people we love. He's trying to destroy our whole world, in fact. We need to go, and we were thinking this temple might have a secret. With all the dimensional traveling going on around here."

"We figured out that this temple is a man," I say, pointing to my knees. "And this part is the knee. Only we don't know what to do, exactly."

"Ah," she says, truly impressed this time. "To reveal the temple's secret, we need an initiate. And I must warn you"—she smirks—"we do things differently in these times. Commoners are not allowed past the second courtyard."

"It's okay," says Tall as he points his thumb at me. "He's King."

"I see," she says, laughing. "Well, my King, because you're the initiate, it is the work you must do within that matters now. Your knees are your foundation. They are also a place of *coming-together*. The joint where your upper leg meets your lower. It is also, symbolically, where the upper kingdom meets the lower kingdom. Where heaven meets earth, the *knot* between the inner and the outer. *He* is the knot, and *ka* is your spiritual self. Together, they make *heka*."

"Like Maestro?" says Tall.

"No, like *magic*," says V.

"You have to be on a threshold, looking at both inside and outside," says Neferet. "Then you become the knot. You make a link, and the energy can flow."

Without thinking, I fall to my knees and close my eyes. I let Neferet's words wash over me. *Where heaven meets earth.* Then another phrase comes to mind, from a while back. *The place where the fading echo meets the rising earth.* Black Herman said that to me once, back in his private grave-yard, to help me make a link between the Realm and the real world. I re-create each step in my imagination, how I placed the Magician's Lost and Found on top of the one in Her-man's mausoleum. *The link. The knot that lets magic flow.*

I feel that surge of energy again, beginning in my feet and charging through my knees.

"Good," says Neferet. "Come."

We follow her through the colonnade where two huge rows of columns run together.

"Must be the femur," says V.

Neferet enters the next section, another open court-yard, surrounded by columns. She stops beneath the main beam resting across the tops of the columns. There are hieroglyphs scrawled on the stone above us.

"It is here," says Neferet, translating the writing. *"The true site of the birth of the king, where he passed his infancy."*

Without thinking, my hand falls to my belly button.

"Yes," she says, noticing my hand. "You are once born, here you are born again, as the sun is born each day."

I feel my old life, my old letdowns, fall away. I release my failures, my disappointment with Marcus, my years of missing Pops. Here and now, I must be born again. I can't let my past define me. I am born each day. *I am always my future, only sometimes my past.*

The surge of magic flows from my knees and resides within my belly.

"Good," says Neferet. "Let's continue."

We march to the end of the courtyard and step into an area where the columns are painted in shades of green and are even more crowded together. There's a god I recognize—Horus, the falcon god, the god of kings, painted on the walls.

"These columns, like papyri plants, are for the papyrus swamp where the god Horus was safeguarded so he could grow and avenge his father," says Neferet.

Too Tall nods to me with raised eyebrows.

"Here the god took a needed rest and a breath. The lungs, the nourishment of the breast."

I hear her and breathe deeply, allowing the flow of energy to come up from my belly, gathering strength.

We follow her through to the next room, the altar and enclave where I failed against Maestro and Marcus betrayed me.

"This is the heart room," says Neferet, "where we feel our loves and our hurts alike. Our hearts are what tell on us when we are judged in the next world. If our hearts are pure, they weigh lighter than a feather on the scales of truth and justice. Do not despair your heartbreaks. They show us who we are."

I touch a hand to my heart. I think about how I brought Maestro his Echo Stone, when Dad had only just gotten it away from him. I let him down. I think about how Pops leaving hurt me, and how much I miss him and want my mom and dad to be back together.

I feel the magical energy surge up from my lungs and through my thumping heart, and I let all those pains go. I realize it only hurts when I cling too tightly, so I choose to release.

We proceed to the next room.

"In this chamber, the five sacred names of the king are written." Neferet points to a wall relief where two figures in profile, wearing crowns, appear to be holding hands and smiling. "This scene is where the queen tells the Amun the name of the divine king to be born."

I raise my hand from my heart to my throat. The flow of energy is bursting through.

"Here is where we awaken the secrets of the temple,

only if each chamber is linked, unblocked, and flowing," says Neferet.

There are several more chambers up ahead. I face the channel of the main hall, where I assume the face and head are.

"If you dream you've lost your voice," I say, remembering the words from the dream book, *"speak your true name when you wake . . ."*

But what's that mean?

What's my true name?

Kingston James, right?

But everyone who knows me and loves me calls me . . .

"KING" bursts from my throat like a river, no dam. I couldn't stop it if I tried. All that energy building up from my feet and my knees and belly into my lungs, chest, and heart comes out my mouth.

A light appears in the chamber up ahead, just as I feel an intense tingling in my face and head.

"By Amun, you've done it!" says Neferet.

We race through the chambers representing the neck and eyes, I guess, and right around the very top of the head, there's a glowing blue portal door.

Just in front, there's a triangular Echo Stone, hovering above a dolerite statue of a cobra.

It rotates at a slow waltz, like a dialed-down version of the cosmos ritual. It's shiny and new, with light refracting through its layered prism.

"*Dream a cobra,*" says Too Tall, "*and you are set for life—19.*"

"So that's why the head was 18, and the cobra was 19," says V. "The cobra—the uraeus." She points to the spot on top of her own head where the uraeus would sit.

A magician can master this stone like how the falcon masters the king. Long Fingers's words reach me from far away in space and time.

The stone has no consciousness. So whatever you put in your mind fills the stone.

"*Go on,*" Neferet whispers to me. "Take it. It must be you, my young King."

I hold up my hand, feeling all this immense power flowing through every inch, every cell of my being. I feel about as big in magic as these colossal statues all around. I don't even mean to call it, but the stone comes to me all on its own. It has that odd sense of balance, the way it's both heavy and light, like all perfect things.

Too Tall grins and gives me an oversized pound and an attaboy pat big enough for Ramses.

I hold the stone in both hands and gaze into its center.

My image emerges like the stone conjured it there. My reflection fills the space of the triangle.

Right. It shows me, because I'm thinking about myself.

So I think about home.

My fingertips tingle on my Realm hand, like a hundred needle pinpricks. I pull it away from the stone, holding my index finger in the air as it blazes like a blue star. I think of how Black Herman made a portal with a fingertip in his graveyard, and I do the same. I trace a rectangle in the air, and light draws from my finger like the ink from a felt-tip pen.

Home, I think, and I look back to my Echo Stone. It doesn't show my face anymore. It shows the James brownstone front stoop, the Thurston Avenue subway station, Not Not Ray's, Cleopatra's Art Supplies full of murals, all dressed with holiday lights and a fresh layer of frost.

V hugs her mom and starts to tear up. I think I know why.

We're coming home.

I LAND ON a cold, hard crystal. Beneath a layer of crystalline crust, there's a familiar usher-worn mauve carpet.

I know it right away.

We're here. Home. The Mercury.

Also known as the Black Rock of Brooklyn, aka HQ for all the strange things that have happened in my life since Pops disappeared from here almost five years ago.

I push up off my chest.

"Stay down," I hear V say in a sharp whisper.

I do as she says. I roll over on my back, trying to get my bearings.

I'm wedged between a row of folded theater chairs

and a balcony wall. I slowly peek over the edge and see the stage below.

And what I see—it's very strange.

There's Maestro-as-Heka. There's Maestro how he was when he chased us through Liberty Hall in Harlem. And there's Marcus wearing the pharaoh's headdress. Guess he was crowned, and now he's here to see his future self finish the job.

They stand in a circle around the crystal monoliths at center stage.

Maestro-as-Heka and Marcus both wear an Echo Stone around their necks. I guess the god-dude let Marcus keep the copy stone he took from me.

"We back," Tall whispers, sitting up on the floor in the row behind me.

"*Shush,*" Veronica shoots back at him.

"Check it," Tall says, pointing over the seat. "Field Goal Head has Sula and her li'l bro on deck."

I look to stage left, and sure enough, Sula and Sol are pinned flat to another pair of crystal monoliths.

"What are they doing here?" I whisper.

"Dude is *their* dad," V reminds me.

"But would your dad pin you against some crystals?" Tall asks.

He's got a point. I mean, Sula didn't want anything to do with her dad, and she could never forgive what he did to Sol. There's no way they're here on their own.

"What time you got, King?" V asks, pointing to the Watch of 13.

I look down. The big hand has lapsed past 12.

"We got less than twenty minutes before we are pancakes," I tell them.

A loud boom erupts from the stage. It sends us all skittering back. The circle of crystals lights up in purple and blue, like a distant galaxy coming to life. Maestro-as-Heka floats up like a hummingbird above the circle. His hands are up at his sides, in imitation of the two hands rising on either side of his headdress. The Echo Stone leaves his neck all on its own, levitates into the air, and begins to spin like a top.

"The time for this accursed world is at an end." His voice thunders through the theater. "My children—all of you will join me in a new realm of existence."

"Are you kidding me?" Sula yells at him. "You kidnapped us!"

"My willful child, you will be glad I did when the deed is done," Maestro replies.

"Glad to be in a world where you've anointed a younger version of *yourself* as the future king?" Sula says.

I look to Marcus and see blankness behind his eyes. He's so skinny, with his narrow shoulders and his bare chest shivering in the cold. Like he's barely big enough to support the copy Echo Stone chained around his neck. He looks scared of himself.

"*Silence.*" Maestro floats back down, his feet touching the stage.

And it's like Sula's mouth has been sealed shut.

"But first, like any good magic performance, we need an audience. One very special guest, who has been here with me from the very beginning."

Maestro tilts the spinning Echo Stone, and a single, intense blue light shoots down from the skies through the hole in the roof. A huge rectangle projects against the dark shadows left of the stage. A glow cuts through the air, forming a giant portal. It's as big as a movie screen, and playing tonight is Nabta Playa. The monoliths stand like the photo negative of the crystal blocks: sand and stone on one side, black crystal on the other. The desert sands roll in the distance, and my pops is trapped against one of the standing stones, right where we left him last.

"My former friend once shared the dream of creating a better reality for ourselves, my children. We are all here now to witness the Great Shift."

Former friend. Yeah, right. This is about their rivalry. Maestro just wants Pops to watch him win.

Pops . . .

I look down from the balcony into Nabta Playa. Pops sits in the sands with his legs stretched out before him. His head is down, and I can barely see his eyes.

Nabta Playa. Where the ritual was done and where it will be undone.

I tap V and whisper, "I think we can undo this. But not here—we do it *there*." I point to the portal for Nabta Playa.

"Explain," whispers Tall.

"Maestro has to use *his* Echo Stone in all three echoes. Once in the alpha, once in the new timeline, in Egypt, and once here in prime. If we can switch out Maestro's Echo Stone and get it to Pops, he can free himself and reverse the very first ritual," I say, my words coming out fast.

"Um, good idea, King," says Tall.

"Can't we just slip your pops the one you just picked up?" asks V. "I mean, that was no walk in the temple."

I look down at the Echo Stone around my neck. Images flicker in its center. Black Herman's Cabinet of Souls, the Magician's Lost and Found, and his coffin out in Woodlawn in the Osiris pose. All portals, I realize, doorways into more worlds that open up with just a thought. I see Black Herman's performance at Liberty Hall, young Marcus and Pops walking the busy streets of Echo City, my pop's magic battle with Maestro right here in this building, and then I see stars rotate in the night sky, and the silhouette of the falcon forms as if outlined in starlight.

The words of my father and Long Fingers ring in my ear.

The falcon is invisible.

Our powers are invisible.

Master this stone like how the falcon masters the king.

I imagine Maestro staring into the stone for the first time, and the power he saw within himself. Whatever he saw, whatever vision of a better world, he became obsessed. The stone showed him too much, and it took him over. The power of his stone is what started this and the only thing that can end it.

I pull my eyes away and see V and Tall staring at me.

"Thought we lost you there," Tall says.

"Only Maestro's stone can undo what he started," I say. "It has to be the one that Maestro used at Nabta Playa." My eyes fall to that Echo Stone, spinning above center stage. "We have to get that stone to my pops."

V looks up at the two of us. "Quiet." She closes her eyes like she's meditating. "I think we have more help down there than we think."

"What's happening? What are you doing, V?" Tall says.

"It's what Sol is doing," V says. "I think he's like me—he can hear us. He can hear my thoughts. And I can hear his."

We peek to see Sol turn his head toward us. It's hardly a glance, but enough to acknowledge that we've got allies on the ground.

I realize that Sol and V were both born to moms who are echoes from the Realm. Only difference is that Sol's mom drained him and scrambled him. She didn't protect him, like V's mom. I wonder if he's able to see all that in V's thoughts, now that V knows. Or maybe he's always known?

"What's he saying?" Tall asks.

V stares hard toward Sol. "He's going to distract him," she says.

I nod and tap the Echo Stone around my neck. "Let's see how Maestro likes a fair fight."

Maestro-as-Heka starts chanting the words of the ancients.

"The sky trembles. The earth quakes before him. The Magician is Maestro. Maestro possesses magic."

There's another eruption, like the Mercury is now a volcano spewing waves of light through the massive hole in the roof. The crash is so loud, you'd think someone demoed a building. Blue light bursts down from the open heavens, and the domed roof of the Mercury is *gone*, blasted up into the sky, truly gone this time.

"*I am 'if-he-wishes-he-does,'*" Maestro-as-Heka continues.

"Father, wait," we hear in a small voice.

In the echo of the crash of the departed roof, that voice would be easy to miss.

But we just catch it.

And so does Maestro.

Tall and I shoot to Veronica.

Did Sol just speak?

Maestro-as-Heka is also shocked by his only son's voice. He looks away from the spinning Echo Stone in the chamber of blue light.

"Yes, my son?" His voice is calm.

"That's your cue," V says to me.

I flex my invisible hand under the white glove and think about the words my father told us back in Nabta Playa. *Our powers are invisible. Our powers are invisible.*

On the stage, Sol pleads with his father. "Please free us. We will come with you, but let us say goodbye to the only world we know."

This stops Maestro-as-Heka. For a moment he almost looks human. He leans in toward Sol.

"Of course. You are free, son," he says.

Sula and Sol slide off the crystals and slump to the floor.

"You will soon forget this world. It will just be a bad dream. Where we are going and the future we will make there will be beyond what you can imagine."

As he speaks, Veronica gives me a look like, *What are you waiting for?*

I hold my Echo Stone in my gloved hand and let it soar down toward the stage, like passing the salt along a slick dinner table.

Our powers are invisible. Our powers are invisible.

I've crushed cans with this hand, I've flown to the top of temples and floated back down, but this is another level—*stealing a stone of immortality from the god of magic.*

I calm my breath, push all those thoughts aside, and recall the power I felt in the Egyptian temple. *There is nothing but myself. And these two stones.*

I can feel my hand now, like I'm touching the spinning Echo Stone. I'm so focused I can't even hear what Sol is saying to his father, but I know he is buying us time.

I get my Echo Stone so it's lined up directly with Maestro's spinning stone.

Spinning stone? Okay, it's got to spin. Stone, I think as a command, *spin.*

And it spins.

Now for the other stone. I call to it, and with Maestro-as-Heka distracted, it flies to me like a hard throw from shortstop to first base.

I've got it. It slaps into my hand, and I let out a little laugh of success.

"*Amazing*, King! Now get it to your dad!" says V.

I was so focused on the swap, I almost forgot. I take another breath and start to guide the stone back down.

Then my heart sinks, and I nearly lose my invisible grip on the hovering stone. As the stone passes by the two alternate Maestros onstage, I make eye contact with young Marcus. He stands next to the older version of himself, from Liberty Hall. His chest and arms are covered with hieroglyphs. His eyes cut through me like a laser, the stone hovering inches above the banister of the balcony.

His eyes drift over to his future self, Maestro-as-Heka, chanting and floating like a demon god at center stage.

I stare at Marcus. Once you get past the headdress and the ancient tattoos, there's the kid we met over pizza in 1984. He doesn't want this. He sees the monster his future self will become. He looks back up at us with a nod, as if to say, *Whatever you're doing to stop him, I'm not getting in the way.*

Then he glances offstage. Saying nothing. Doing nothing.

Attaboy, Marcus.

I push the stone through the air and fling it down toward the open portal. It lands in the sand between Dad's feet. The white of a smile flashes within his beard.

I check Maestro-as-Heka. He's returned to the ritual, hands held to the spinning stone like everything is according to his plan.

Whew.

I feel like an elephant just lifted his foot off my chest.

V and Tall are staring at me like I just walked on water.

"What, didn't believe in me?"

Tall shakes his head. "Thought I was gonna pass out just watching you."

From below, the chant resumes. *"I have come that I may take possession of my throne and that I may receive my dignity,"* incants Maestro-as-Heka. *"For to me belonged the universe before you came into being. Descend, you who have come in the end. I am Heka."*

My Echo Stone spins and spins at Maestro's command. But he doesn't seem to detect that it isn't his. Then the stone stops, and it feels like the world around us spins instead.

The very tip of the stone shoots a bright light up into

the heavens. It goes and goes like it won't stop until it reaches the stars.

I check the portal to Nabta Playa. Dad is free. Maestro's Echo Stone is now spinning above the desert stone circle.

"Heka!" calls the adult Maestro, snarling like when he chased us through Liberty Hall. "Preston—look at Preston!"

But Maestro-as-Heka is too entranced to hear him.

"Heka!" he calls.

Always checking for my pops, isn't he? I think.

Adult Maestro looks at the people around him in the crystal circle. There's the daughter and son he will one day have but has never met. There's himself as a teenager, who's not okay with this anymore. I wonder, will he join his young self and break ranks with the god-man?

Adult Maestro lunges at Marcus. He snatches the Echo Stone by the chain and yanks it over his head.

"Maestro," says V. "He took the kid's stone!"

"That is so like him," says Tall.

"He sees it going wrong," I say. "Wants something for his own."

Maestro-as-Heka's eyes open with a blue, glowing rage. "Something's not right!" he declares.

"Yes," says adult Maestro as he places Marcus's chain around his own neck. "Preston—" he starts.

278

"My stone—it's not working," says Maestro-as-Heka.

Because it's my stone, you fool.

"But, Heka, look—*Preston!*" shouts adult Maestro.

Maestro-as-Heka sees into the portal to Nabta Playa. "No!"

Dad is chanting, the night desert sky is lit up, the stars are spinning and blurring like lights in the subway tunnel.

Pops says, *"You gods, go down and come upon the blacker parts. For I am a magician."*

"He's realigning everything," says Veronica. "Your dad—he's making things right! He's calling the comet back to that echo."

Dad stands beside the spinning Echo Stone. No floating, no chanting anymore, just the revolutions of the pyramid-shaped stone slowing as Maestro's spell is undone.

"Nooo!" Maestro-as-Heka cries, his hands balled into fists. A tremendous surge of power is coming from him. An outpouring of rage and grief and shock so intense, I feel it tremble in my guts. A scream pierces every inch of crystal as his spinning Echo Stone screeches like a kettle.

The crystal cathedral around us glows purple. The high-pitched sound grows deafening.

There are three explosions, popping one after the other like blown stage lights.

The stone above the crystal stage explodes.

The stone around adult Maestro's neck explodes.

The stone in Nabta Playa explodes.

With Pops standing behind it.

No. NO. NO!

"Dad, Dad," I cry.

Pops slumps over, holding his stomach. Blood seeps through his fingers.

A piece of Maestro's stone has impaled him.

I glance to the stage, where someone is howling. There's adult Maestro, who only just put that stone around his neck thinking he had the key to immortality when it blew out his chest. He slumps over and stops moving. His body turns to pure crystal, like an ice sculpture.

"Um, King?" I hear Veronica.

Everything about me is glowing blue. It feels like my entire body is my hand. There's no separation anymore. Spirit and body are one. The cosmos and ground are one. Like I can touch the skies and the oceans and the depths of the earth. I think I'm floating. But it's as easy as walking. I can sense every inch of crystal. Every speck, every particle. They're there like the hairs on my arm. I can make them stand. I can make them move. I can throw them. I can shoot them at Maestro-as-Heka.

With a twist of my neck, I rip the crystal monoliths from the stage floor and send them flying. They crash into Maestro. I rip more crystals out of the Mercury and hurl them. Crystals in the shape of cones, cut like jagged glass, or like massive boulders. He destroys some. Some, he doesn't. Those slash at him, cut him, bruise him. He's falling backward, stumbling toward the portal for Nabta Playa. I see a light as if my eyes are glowing bright purple. The power of the Realm surges through me.

I summon every little molecule of crystal in the theater, gather them into one colossal ball and smash it into Maestro-as-Heka. I send the whole mass crashing through the portal.

King, I hear. *King, it's okay, please. You're scaring me. Scaring us.*

I look down. I realize what I must look like. I am floating about twenty feet above the orchestra seats. And the theater, it's not covered in crystal anymore.

There's V, showing me her biggest eyes. She's talking to me in my head.

It's okay. Come down, please.

She has an arm around Sula, who's crying in her shoulder. Tall has his one arm around Sol and the other around Marcus. He looks at me like he looked at the comet on the rooftop a few loops back. I realize he's trying to protect them . . . from me.

"*Wha*-what did I do?" I wonder, and lower myself to the stage floor, which is once more made of wood. "I could have destroyed everyone."

"You almost did. I've never seen you like that. You were, like, possessed," Tall says.

"King, look," V says.

I follow her gaze into the portal for Nabta Playa.

Amid the standing stones, Maestro lies flat on the ground, his Heka headdress half buried in the sands. He's beneath a huge slab of crystal, and he can't move.

Dad is also on the ground. He's leaning against a stone monolith again, but this time he's not chained to it. He's bleeding.

"Dad, no," I say, and tears flood my face.

"Wait," says V. "Look!"

A figure comes up behind Pops.

A very familiar silhouette wearing a Prince Albert coat with a pyramid shape attached to a chain around his neck.

Black Herman.

He takes the chain off over his head. He places it on my dad instead, resting the last Echo Stone on his chest.

Black Herman glances at Maestro on the ground. He just shakes his head.

Then he leans over, picks up my dad, and hauls him over his shoulder.

He looks at me. Or he looks at us, I can't quite tell.

He smiles and winks, and then takes a running start, jumping toward us.

And like that, the portal *vanishes*.

We're all on the stage. Alone.

Just six kids.

No portal, no crystal, no stones, no adults.

No Pops.

At least not here.

And at least there *is* here.

Our Echo City. Moving forward in time.

I look into the stars through the missing roof of the old Mercury Theater.

No one says anything for a few heartbeats. The quiet is so intense, it's terrifying. And I realize it's snowing through the open roof. The snow blankets the city and muffles its noise so it feels like you can even hear the flakes as they fall. Only the snow—it's *black as coal*.

V looks up to the sky. "From when Maestro blasted the roof off," she says. "What goes up . . ."

"Black crystal," says Tall with a shrug. "Black snow."

"It's beautiful," says Sula.

"You guys okay?" I ask.

"We're okay," says V. "You okay?"

"I think so." *But I really don't know.*

"What was that—with Herman?" asks Tall.

"He—he closed it," I say. "He gave Pop his Echo Stone. And he closed the portal."

"You okay, King?" V asks again, like she wants the truth this time.

"He took my dad, and—V, you think he's going to be okay?"

"Your dad?" V asks. "Yeah, King. I think so."

Then Tall sees something on the ground and bends down to get it.

It's a hunk of black crystal, about the size of my fist. As far as I can see, the only bit left from what was once the Black Rock of Brooklyn.

"Looks like you missed this one, King." He hands it to me.

I examine the rock, its black heart and purple striations catching moonlight.

And I pass the rock to Marcus. "Um, Marcus? I think you're going to need to keep this close."

"KING," **MOM CRIES** when she sees me at the door.

She takes me in her arms and squeezes with everything she has. I hold on to her extra long and go limp in her arms. Like the way she used to hold me when I'd fall asleep on the couch and she'd carry me upstairs to bed.

Her eyes well up with tears.

I'm *so* glad to see her.

Other than that, I feel exhausted and empty. I just want sleep.

V hugs my mom next as Ma eyes the rest of the crew lining the stoop.

"Um, Ma? Is it okay if Too—Eddie—Sula, Sol, and Marcus stay for dinner?"

"Um, oh, hi, everyone," she says. "Nice to see you again, Sula. Sol." She nods. "Eddie, call your parents. And Marcus?" she says with a lift in her voice.

"Long story," I say.

"I'd love to hear it. Kids, you can hang in the living room, how's that? And, King, come with me."

That last part she says like the crack of a whip.

"You too, Veronica."

We follow Ma into the kitchen like convicts awaiting sentencing.

I think about what Ma's been through. We've been missing since last night. I never came home, for the first time ever. The last anyone saw of us was when we told Uncle Crooked Eye we were going to get something to eat after the Nets game.

Anger, relief, frustration, and love are all balled up into one expression on her face.

"I'm sorry, Ma."

"I know, it's a long story. Maybe I tell you mine before you tell me yours?" she says.

V and I look at each other, a bit caught off guard.

"So last night, we were waiting for you all to get home from the Nets game," she starts in. "Then your *always-dependable* uncle Heyward shows up here without you."

Her words ooze with sarcasm as she pours the contents of a Tupperware container marked *Crooked Chili* into a pot on the stove.

"Sure, I was annoyed but figured you were in good hands with V. I mean, I was young in Brooklyn once, too. So, I let it go."

Ma slowly stirs Crooked's chili, and we're hanging on her every word.

"But then it got *real* late and you still hadn't showed up," she continues. "We had closed up the shop and counted the cash register, and you better believe I was livid with Heyward. How could he leave you kids out there? But deep down, I knew it wasn't his fault. Something else was up.

"I called Not Not Ray's. Caught Matteo just before he left for the night. But no dice. He hadn't seen you three."

She tastes the chili.

"So then I called Eddie's parents. They were up and sick with worry. They were about to call *me*. It was the last thing we wanted to do, but now we had to call the police. Then I got a knock on the front of the store. Guess who it was."

"No clue."

"An agent from the federal Omega Team," she says, stirring the chili again. "Nice guy in a pair of loafers. He was just standing there looking like he'd seen a ghost.

"He told me they had an *incident* at the Mercury Theater. A break-in. And the rest, well, I'm sure you already
know—a mirror, a skull, cards, a pistol, a beam of light
from the cosmos. Par for the course, right? He thought I
wouldn't believe any of it. But I believed every word."

Ma wasn't worried about us getting kidnapped or getting into trouble out there in Brooklyn. She knew we had
gone to the Realm.

Long Fingers and Crooked Eye come barreling down
the stairs.

"So I made these two yahoos come clean," says Mom.
"They told me everything."

My uncles see us and stop in their tracks.

"Oh, thank the stars, you all made it back!" Long Fingers says.

He hugs Veronica.

Then we all get in on a big family hug.

All I can see is that teenage version of Long Fingers,
with his tank top and swagger.

I toss Crooked Eye the satchel of coins, or at least
what's left of them.

"So that change came in handy," I say.

"I figured it might," he replies. "You must have gone on
quite a grand tour."

"Yeah, and we met someone *else*," V says. I watch her lips move in slow motion as she speaks, like every sound is a trip around the sun.

She doesn't need to say another word. The woman's presence is written on Long Fingers's face.

Neferet.

Mom.

"Why didn't you tell me?" V asks.

Her father slumps like a balloon deflating.

"You met her," he says.

V nods. "How could you never say anything?"

"I loved her so much and you reminded me so much of her, I just . . . *couldn't*. You were so little, you still fit right in my forearm. We noticed something was wrong. It was Herman who explained it to us. He appeared to Preston in Granddad's old mirror. Said we had to bring her back where she came from. He even lent us his Echo Stone, for the trip, through the Lost and Found. We went back to her temple, said goodbye, and haven't spoken her name since. I couldn't. It, um, it hurt too much."

V holds a steady gaze at her father until he looks away.

"I'm sorry, Veronica," he growls. "I should have told you. I was weak. You deserve better."

V wraps her arms around his thick neck and squeezes.

There's so much pain there, I realize. He lost his one love, and he was never the same after that. Just kept to himself and his inventions, all of that feeling locked up tight.

I look to Mom and think about how she and Long Fingers both lost their loves to the Realm. And then I went there, again, and she thought she might never see me, again.

Just like Pops.

"I saw him," I tell her. "I saw Dad, Ma."

She looks up from the table.

"We talked and we looked at the stars, just like we used to."

Ma is holding back tears.

"He didn't make it back. But I think he's okay, Ma. Wherever he is. I know he's okay."

I WAKE UP in a cold sweat, expecting to hear the *thum-da-doom* of the subway. Instead it's the *beep beep beep* of a garbage truck backing up outside, honking horns, the sweet sounds of jackhammers and the *coo*s of pigeons perched outside my window. It's like a symphony to me. Life has moved on, and it's Christmas morning. After an unending weekend, I've never been so happy to see Monday. A smile creeps across my face as I stretch my legs and bury my head in the pillow.

Downstairs, King's Cup is coming to life. A Nat King Cole carol blares from the speakers behind the counter. The Christmas tree is lit up in the corner. Crooked Eye has touched it up with a dusting of black snow to honor our big night. He kept a couple of black snowballs in the freezer. He comes around the corner in a baker's apron with a fruitcake he's about to throw into the oven.

The smell of baked goods and coffee hits my nose.

"Hello, sleepyface," he says.

I stop him.

"Please come up with a new morning greeting, Unc," I say.

He lets out a monster laugh and points me toward the table ahead.

"Fresh chocolate croissants hot out of the oven to the right, my famous banana bread to the left. What can I get ya?"

"Uh, one of each," I say.

"Perfect! The choice of a king. Have a seat," Crooked says as he saunters behind the counter.

Long Fingers, Ma, and V sit by the tree near the window. A few gifts and wrapping paper are spread around the table.

"Good morning, King," Ma says.

I give Ma a hug, holding on for a few extra seconds. As I sit down, I dap Long Fingers.

"Sorry we couldn't wait to open a few," Ma says.

There's a box sitting open in front of V.

"What'd ya get?"

"A very special gift from Santa Fingers over there," my cousin says.

She pulls out a wooden box, and inside is a beautiful ivory headdress with a black obsidian crystal cobra on top, looking straight out of ancient Egypt.

"It was one of hers," V says. "I miss her already."

Ma squeezes my hand and glances out the window.

"Look at that, it's opening time, and the customers are already lining up."

"Ma, you good if V and I go meet with Tall in a bit?" I ask. "We gotta show Marcus how little Not Not Ray's has changed."

"Sure, King. Just promise me—*no other dimensions.*"

V chuckles. "Auntie got jokes!"

⚡

OUT ON RICKS Street, I hear Tall's laugh before I see him.

He's walking with Marcus. "Sorry, I was trying to explain to Marcus how a cellie works. This guy is hilarious. I showed him modern video games just now—blew his mind!"

Tall's outfitted Marcus in a Yankees Starter jacket from his smallest cousin that's still a few sizes too big. I see the chain around Marcus's neck, and I know what's at the end of it under his shirt. *The last Black Rock of BK.*

"So, we hitting Not Not Ray's?" Marcus asks. "There was no Brooklyn-style pizza in Egypt."

"Yup, it's a Christmas Day tradition in the James family," I say.

"And Matteo's is open three hundred sixty-five days a year!" Tall adds.

"Yeah, just wanna make one stop on the way," I say. "One person I want to say hello to on Christmas."

We turn left down Broken Jade Junction, and there's the mural of Black Herman's Private Graveyard. Sol has been busy the last few days. There's a new addition. A statue of Black Herman carved out of black rock stands in front of the mausoleum.

Thank you, Black Herman.

There's someone I know well standing in the grassy lawn of the graveyard. I can almost see the wind blowing in his salt-and-pepper beard. Dad wears Black Herman's old Echo Stone around his neck now.

I reach my gloved hand to the wall and feel a spike of energy.

Pops.

Merry Christmas.

ACKNOWLEDGMENTS

FOR THE MOST part, we wrote this book during the 2020 pandemic. It was a strange time. Still is. We hunkered down with our families and did our best to keep our kids safe and their imaginations alive. Time moved in a different way. We worked in dusty garages in the middle of the night and screened-in porches in the middle of the woods. Our kids climbed all over us; we fed them, changed them, put them to sleep—all while the three of us weaved this story together from thousands of miles apart. As much as we thought we were protecting them, we realize now they were also protecting us. They gave us the world back through their eyes. As the world came to a stop, we could finally see what they were seeing. We are beyond grateful for that experience.

Many thanks for the insight, patience, and occasional hilarious comments from our editing team of Stacey Barney and Caitlin Tutterow. Jane Startz—none of this happens without you! Thanks to Ashley Spruill and Megan Beatie for getting the word out on our first book. Much love to all the local bookstores that showed us support while they were all holding on by a thread through this crazy time. We need to support them now more than ever! Also, thank you to the online community that mushroomed up all over the country in support for Kingston (with a special shout to Ainara's Bookshelf for the endless creative reviews!).

We met some great magicians as we rolled out the first book. Thanks to Justin Willman and Eric Jones, who talked magic with us and made us feel good that we captured the spirit of their incredible craft. Thanks to all our friends who've taken the time to read our words and indulge in long conversations about them. Shout to our HQs on both coasts, St. Francis College's MFA program in Brooklyn and SunnyBoy Pasadena, for always giving us a place of refuge. Lastly, thanks to Kingston, Veronica, and Too Tall for letting us take this adventure with you. It's been a ride, and we can't wait to see where it goes next!